Likely Voters

A Speculative Political Novel

By Blain Hamilton

To Americans throughout our country who are compelled to make a difference...

and to best friends everywhere who support each other through thick and thin.

A Note to Readers

While this is a work of fiction, it was inspired by real political events that occurred between 2016 and 2020. To this end, newspaper and magazine references are included at the beginning of some chapters and are intended to provide a context for the fictionalized events occurring in Likely Voters. These references are meant to be read in parallel with the text.

"*In the face of impossible odds, people who love this country can change it.*"

Barack Obama

"*A vote is like a rifle; its usefulness depends upon the character of the user.*"

Theodore Roosevelt

"*I'm just trying to do my part to save the world.*"

J. Cornell Michel

... "*make sure you get out and vote on Nov. 28,*"

DJTrump October 12, 2016

Table of Contents

Prologue - November 2, 2020

The dark figure quietly approached the door to the association office. Even at this hour, it was risky to be out. Anyone could be up at 4:00 in the morning and looking out their window. The intruder entered the access code and soundlessly opened the door. Luckily, they had not upgraded security to biometrics yet.

Inside, a quick search revealed the server and within moments the mistake that could have doomed the plan was identified. Just as he had thought - this would have been a disaster. Only his experience as a data center manager allowed him to anticipate the need to account for audio capture as well as video. Re-directing this feed to a temporary streaming audio server would close the loop and keep anyone working in the office from being aware of the diversion. The question was – could they keep it in place for three days?

It was an audacious plan - he had never heard of anyone trying this kind of thing before. Had it not been for overhearing the phone call, he would have been in the dark like everyone else. They had thought of almost everything and with this last technical fix, the plan could actually work.

Suddenly the security monitor from the front gate blared the voice of Logan, the night security guard. "Where are you headed, who are you visiting today?"

A scratchy old voice replied "Our tee time is on the Palmer course at 6:00. We're first off today, wanted to get breakfast and some strong coffee before teeing off."

"I think you managed to beat everyone – maybe even the clubhouse cooks" said Logan. "The groundskeepers are arriving so the clubhouse will be open soon. You might have to wait another ten minutes or so, but you should be able to get your bacon and eggs before your tee time. Pull ahead gentlemen and welcome to Leisure Falls.

After another minute, his racing heart was finally beating normally again, and he quickly adjusted the feed so that the rewiring would not be noticed. This should work unless someone really knows their way around a streaming audio server, but he doubted anyone here would have the expertise. He wrapped his tools and placed them back in his backpack, exited the data center and carefully crept out the office door. He snapped off his gloves and pocketed them for disposal later. No fingerprints. He donned a bird watching hat and binoculars and headed down the path to the pond. There he would join the other bird watchers for sunrise and another day in retirement paradise.

Chapter 1 – November 2016

"Donald Trump is urging his supporters to vote on Election Day — but he got one key fact wrong. In the opening moments of a rally Tuesday night in Palm Beach City, Florida, Trump told the crowd to "make sure you get out and vote, Nov. 28."

The problem with that advice? Election Day is actually Nov. 8."

Little did we know at that time what an epic disaster we were heading toward. With Hillary up 3-7 points in the polls political analysts were predicting that she would be the winner and the first female president of the United States.

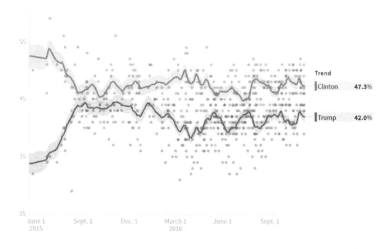

Huffington Post showed polls of likely voters predicting Clinton ahead.[1]

But on November 8th, Linda watched the returns on NBC and knew by 7:00 that things were not going as predicted. On the way home from the

---

[1] https://elections.huffingtonpost.com/pollster/2016-general-election-trump-vs-clinton

train station, David had said, "She's lost Pennsylvania." By the time they turned on the news, political pundits were reserving judgement, but the mood was already grim.

Linda went to the kitchen for her second glass of Pinot Noir to go with their dinner of turkey chili and corn bread. Even though November is technically still fall, Chicago had already been below freezing and had seen the first accumulating snowfall last week. These dark and cold evenings at the beginning of the winter were perfect for a crockpot dinner. David and Linda had begun to enjoy quiet evenings by the fire watching a favorite show and reading. Wilson, their golden retriever joined them on the couch, and this would be the family routine for most of the winter.

"This does not look good at all", Linda said as she flipped the channel to Fox news to see what their coverage was like. "Here we were ready to celebrate the first woman president of the United States and this crazy, unbelievable turn of events is starting to become real." She checked her phone to see if any encouraging news was available. "I can't image how this could be happening."

"It all depends on who shows up to vote." David said. "There are a lot of voters who are not happy with their own situation. Jobs, finances, housing values - all the people who have not seen a recovery and are still having a tough time are more energized to vote and they are saying – We want change".

Linda mused over their own situation and knew that they were among the lucky ones who were doing fine. They both had stable jobs and minimal debt. Even as they neared retirement age, they both were still lucky enough to be in good health. Of course, their efforts to live a healthy lifestyle were part of the reason for this. When she was young, Linda's mother had said certain things that had stuck and become part of her own personal philosophy on life. "Sleep is sacred", "Everything in moderation", "Just a taste, not a bellyful". This had turned out to be good advice and now it was just the way Linda and David did things. Even though they had busy and demanding jobs, they were manageable and enabled them to keep a regular sleep pattern, eat healthy, and work out at the gym at least twice a week. Linda felt fortunate to have reached this age without having health problems. Her biggest goal was now to reach 65 and get on Medicare before anything really went wrong.

Finally, at 10:00 they decided to call it a night and try to forget about the result that looked inevitable – Tom Driscoll was going to be President of the United States. How could this have happened? What would the next four years be like? It was hard to understand how so many people were voting for someone who clearly had no desire to work on problems of regular working people.

The next day was Linda's regular Wednesday lunch call with Bev. They had both been watching the returns of the election and were more than dismayed with the results. Linda and Bev were friends from high school, college roommates and then remained connected on through married life. Because they had lived only 12 minutes from each other for over 40 years, they had the unusual gift to continue to be part of each other's lives. They were much more than ordinary friends. Over the years they had been through many life milestones together: weddings, children, baptisms, graduations, deaths, children's weddings. The full circle of life.

All of this added up to a deep understanding of how the other would think and act. Knowing in a way that only develops after decades of sharing everything.

Linda was so sure of Bev and being able to depend on her for anything, she felt they were closer than most sisters. They saw eye-to-eye on most things in fact – Linda didn't know of anything on which they took dramatically different viewpoints.

Linda and David had been steadily preparing for retirement. It was only a few years away now and the question of where to live (it was too expensive to stay in Chicago) and what they wanted to do in retirement was a regular topic of conversation. Although many retirees headed south, Linda and David did not want to live in the south year-round. Of course, the idea of escaping to warm weather in the winter was appealing. Linda did not particularly like the idea of missing the change of seasons or leaving everything and everyone from a lifetime of living behind. They discussed a plan that combined the best of both worlds. While still working they would keep their home in the Chicago suburbs, but gradually they would begin moving to the lake house they had purchased in Lake Geneva, Wisconsin. Luckily, both had rewarding careers and enjoyed their work. They would be able to do anything they wanted in retirement as long as they were healthy, "the world was their oyster".

"Why would so many people vote for Driscoll when he obviously doesn't care about them? He won't do what he is promising. This was the biggest con job ever", said Bev.

"This makes absolutely no sense," Linda agreed. "Every day I wake up and can't believe this has happened. It just seems like this can't be real. What a nightmare! I have decided never to watch MSNBC again. How could the "experts" have been so wrong?"

Over the next three years, Linda and Bev continued to wonder about the election and where it was leading the country. There were a lot of theories being discussed on TV news shows. In fact, over the years, political science experts and amateurs alike analyzed all the theories and arrived at a few main conclusions:

The vote was the result of a slow to recover economy that had left less educated people with fewer options for jobs in a new global and technology driven economy. At the same time, voters were also motivated not only by economic hardship, but by the simple fact that they felt threatened by change to their way of life. This type of change led people to feel nostalgic for "the good old days" and to look for others like themselves to bond with and a desire for their own group to once again be dominant and in control. Driscoll voters felt their status in society was threatened and not just economically, it went much deeper than that.

These truths had been hammered into everyone's head over the last three years. What was a shock on the morning after the election had become a daily nightmare. Over these three years there was no change to voters' views and feelings. In fact, voters seemed even more entrenched in their positions. As 2019 began and candidates began to announce their intention to run, it looked like the 2020 election was going to be as big a fight as 2016 had been. This time the Democrats had more than a dozen candidates vying to be chosen to run against the incumbent. Despite investigations into improprieties with Russia, pardons offered to Driscoll cronies, the immigration fiasco, and a host of other problems of the last three years, it seemed that Driscoll was in a very strong position to win the presidency again. It certainly was depressing.

. . . . . .

The bedside alarm gradually started to brighten. After years of commuting to the city, Linda had finally found a way to get up at 5:30 am without being jolted out of bed by a blaring wake-up. Just last week she had put the finishing touches on a makeover of their master bedroom. The right lighting, plants, and music all contributed to the calming atmosphere. She had discovered an alarm clock that used light as the wake-up. Just like a sunrise, the light gradually brightened and then music came on. Linda had found that she usually awakened by the light alone, so this meant that David was not impacted by her getting up an hour earlier than him. As spring approached and the days got longer, the early morning was naturally light, and she didn't even need to use an alarm.

Before the music came on, Linda shut off the alarm, pulled on some sweats and peered into the bathroom mirror before heading to the kitchen. Her short brown highlighted hair framed her face almost perfectly even first thing in the morning. Only a quick touch-up was needed to straighten the back - finished off with a couple of squirts of hairspray.

Morning was one of her favorite times of day, even if it was awfully early. An hour of quiet time to read, have her first cup of coffee and spend some time with Wilson, their golden retriever, got her day off to a peaceful start. Wilson was a new addition to the family, keeping their long string of golden retrievers intact.

Linda took a few slow stretches and gradually pulled her 5'3-inch frame into a full overhead reach. After a few minutes to wake up her muscles, she took another brief look in the mirror. A lifetime of regular exercise, sleep and a relatively healthy diet was delivering benefits. Linda looked younger than her age and at the same time consequences – she had problems with a bunion on her right foot and her knee aches and pains-- had forced her to redesign her exercise routine. Overall, she felt good each morning, so she really had no complaints.

Recently Linda had worked with her colorist to plan out how to gradually show gray in her dark hair. Back in the days when she worked in the business world, she had kept her hair darker, but now that she worked in academia where gray hair was accepted, she had decided to gradually go gray. Having to constantly color hair was not only expensive, it was time consuming and conforming to the view that women needed to look younger. She had now decided that she would act more in line with her own views on what is practical and not conform to the notion, still accepted by many women, that women need to try to look younger.

Along with this change, Linda had quit wearing the corporate suits and heels and adopted a new wardrobe more fitting with the need to commute for 3 hours to get to and from campus. After all, weren't heels just short of the practice of binding feet? Although the new "Me Too" movement sometimes went too far and still had some unexplained gaps, it did look like the younger women were making progress in the shoe department. Few women now wore heels to work these days. The new trend for casually comfortable, yet stylish sneakers was perfect, and Linda had black and metallic pairs that could cover all occasions and outfits.

Wilson was patiently waiting in the kitchen with his stuffed frog in his mouth and tail wagging. What a good buddy Wilson was turning out to be. They had adopted him in March and he already was blending in with the routine. Linda had thought they would get a smaller dog this time as it might be easier to handle walking and bringing a 25-pound dog to visit friends and family. But, the opportunity for Wilson came along and despite his 107 pounds, they jumped at the chance to have another golden retriever.

Linda sat on the bottom stairs and Wilson came close for some morning pets and conversation. His tail wagged quickly, and he slid to the floor and rolled over for tummy scratching. Linda was reminded again of a phrase her Dad said when they got their last dog, "they quicken your step and remind you of the goodness of God's creation". It was so true, and Wilson was living proof of this.

The coffee was brewing, and Linda poured a cup while she prepared her oatmeal and strawberries for breakfast. Today would be the first warm day of spring – reaching 60 degrees so she put some of her plants out on the patio to enjoy the fresh air and sunshine. She had been conscientiously watering the new plants since she started the seeds about a month earlier. Now she had marigolds, green pepper plants, basil, parsley and morning glories ready to plant in the yard as soon as there was no more danger of frost.

Wilson joined Linda on the patio and quietly sniffed his favorite spots. He had his own morning routine which included some time watching the sun rise and listening to the birds. After this morning meditation, they both went back in to enjoy breakfast.

This was when Linda's peaceful start could be abruptly interrupted by looking at the news feeds on her phone. Facebook, New York Times, Crain's Chicago Business, USA Today – whatever you read it was all the same for the last three years. Lots of bad news. Since the election of Tom Driscoll, every day brought a new outrage of some kind. Immigrants, tariffs, taxes, climate change – every issue had bad news and seemed to be contributing to a decline in the overall situation impacting the everyday lives of regular people.

Linda and David both stayed aware of current issues and news and frequently discussed them, but they had decided it was not worth their peace of mind to watch any news on TV. That could easily become a habit that sucked up hours of time and for what? It just made you miserable with all the bad news. Linda now limited herself to ten minutes of reading news on her phone just to see the headlines so that she was aware of any new catastrophe, but then she firmly zipped the phone into her briefcase.

Upstairs, the sounds of the shower coming on indicated that David was up. "Listen Wilson", Linda whispered, "David is up". Wilson responded by cocking his head to one side and holding his breath to listen. His tail wagged as the clues computed – David was up and soon would be coming downstairs – another source of pets and a walk down the block to sniff each mailbox – Wilson's version of reading the mail. As the next twenty minutes unfolded, the pace of the morning picked up. David pulled his lunch together; Linda checked her Ventra app to ensure that she still had tickets ready to be used. They had cooked over the weekend so it would be leftover chicken for dinner. Both said a quick goodbye to Wilson and headed out the door.

Chapter 2 - June 2019

WASHINGTON – President Donald Trump on Wednesday appeared to blame current immigration laws – and Democrats' refusal to change them – for the drowning death of a father and his young daughter as they tried to cross the Rio Grande river to get into the United States.

"People are running through the Rio Grande," he told reporters on the White House South Lawn. "If we had the right laws ... people won't come up and people won't get killed."

By Natalie Gallón, Ana Melgar and Steve Almasy, CNN, Wed June 26, 2019

Bev disconnected from her weekly Wednesday video chat with Linda feeling vaguely dissatisfied. She looked around her somewhat cluttered kitchen trying to put her finger on exactly what was bothering her. Well, she mused, it was certainly understandable that she would feel unsettled. After all, her life of recent had been a roller coaster of upheaval.

First, the move to Florida—three years ago, after the election. She had allowed herself to be convinced by Harry that unlimited sunshine and golf would make up for a life without the daily presence of her kids and girlfriends, especially her best friend Linda. At the time, it had seemed like the right thing to do. Harry had uncomplainingly worked his whole life and deserved the retirement of his dreams. He had never in their 34 years of marriage insinuated that she should leave the freelance journalist job that she loved for a more lucrative and stable fulltime position.

Leisure Falls had seemed like a great choice -a self-sustaining over 55 retirement community that offered a myriad of golf, tennis and social clubs. The layout, 25 neighborhoods, each with restaurants, shops, movie theaters and banks, each designed to reflect a unique motif, seemed both charming and welcoming. There were forest preserve areas that provided biking and walking trails as well as town squares which acted as social hubs connecting the neighborhoods. Harry and Bev had chosen a 3-bedroom ranch style home in the Harbor Town neighborhood, designed to mimic a New England coastal village. They had anticipated many years of free golf, bike rides and visits from their kids.

Harry's retirement, and their life together, had been cut tragically short by a fatal heart attack a mere six months after moving into Leisure Falls.

She caught her reflection in the hall mirror. A small, disheveled, plump 60-year -old woman frowned back at her. She noted that her dark mop of curly hair could use a trim and perhaps another dose of highlighting to hide the encroaching grey. And if she was being at all honest, she was way overdue for a wardrobe upgrade. The ladies of central Florida were generally arrayed in trendy golf attire, whether they played or not. Her usual garb of LL Bean polos, crop pants, and Teva's were not "up to par". She smiled when she thought of how her daughter Ruthie would often soften her appraising glance once she realized "Mom was doing her best." Comfort usually trumped fashion for Bev.

Sighing heavily, Bev attempted to resist the ever-present urge to descend into despair and self-pity. Leisure Falls was rife with women "of a certain age" living alone, although many were trying mightily to change that situation—the Friday night and Sunday afternoon mixers were highly popular here. But Bev, widowed for more than two years now, missed her old connections up north. She missed the lively debate and easy laughter of her tribe of close friends, women who were fiercely passionate about all the components of their complicated, busy lives. Yes, she had to admit, most conversations did seem to lead to the current dismal political scene and the bombastic, bigoted president who had inexplicably won in 2016. Bev felt her blood pressure rise as she once again, for the thousandth time, shook her head in disbelief that so many had voted for a man who was clearly uninterested in improving anyone's life but his own.

Down here, in the relentlessly sunny days of central Florida, passionate conversation on any subject seem as dry and bleached out as the terrain. Everyone was pleasant enough, but the conversation always seemed to be predictably divided by gender—golf and the booming economy for the fellas, grandchildren and home décor for the gals with occasional digression into the failing health of a neighbor or friend. Of course, this was a frightening subject better to be talked about almost furtively, lest fate be tempted. It was all so pleasant but often bland and superficial. No rousing discussions of the messy and complex issues of immigration or healthcare. Most of the Leisure Falls residents enjoyed the generous healthcare benefits of Medicare. The teeming masses of women and children attempting to cross the Rio Grande for a better life seemed very very far away. These problems which dominated most of the news stations had no place among the orderly, pristine neighborhoods of Leisure Falls, kept that way by a cadre of brown-skinned help. Bev often, somewhat enviously, surmised that this silent army of support staff had lively interactions just out of notice of most residents.

Bev tended to keep her political views to herself in Florida. As a Democrat in a sea of conservatives, she was greatly outnumbered. With the current strong economy and the healthy 401Ks and investment portfolios of her neighbors, Leisure Falls was a powerful Republican voting force. In fact, it had been reported that the community's staunch Republican stance had been a significant factor in the last election. Not many of the 128,000 residents took the time out of a leisure-centered life to contemplate the morality of the present administration's policies. They reasoned that they had worked hard their entire lives to ensure a retirement free of financial worry and had little sympathy for other's hard luck stories.

With one last heavy sigh, Bev squared her shoulders and vowed to reclaim herself. Two and a half years of mourning was enough. Her grief of losing Harry had been overwhelming at times, not to mention the loss of an expectation that they would enjoy many years together. They had spent countless chilly afternoons around their backyard fire pit in Illinois envisioning a retirement filled with golfing, travel, and sunshine. She knew Ruthie and her two sons, Ross and Jason were concerned. The boys loved her unabashedly.

Ruthie, more sensitive, intuited how lonely she was in Florida. Bev knew she needed a change—perhaps a trip or a new project, or even a relocation back north. It all seemed so exhausting. Maybe Linda would have some ideas

At 11:15 Linda stretched her arms, leaned back and looked at the ceiling. She had been working since 7:00 with Wilson quietly lying under the desk. They both stood up and Linda rolled her head in slow circles to counteract the last four hours of looking down at her computer screen. It was time for the "lunch walk". Working from home a couple of days a week allowed Linda to continue her exercise routine involving walking, yoga and the Nordic track machine they had in the basement. Long before anyone had a Fitbit, Linda had been tracking miles, first running, but in the past 5 years she had switched to walking to preserve her knees and feet. Twelve years of tracking had resulted in 9,467 miles so her goal for this year was to break 10,000 miles. When Linda had turned 30, her mother had said, "you can't afford not to exercise" and she had taken this good advice to heart. The only time in her life that she had not regularly exercised was in her final year of earning her PhD when there simply was no time. Before and since then it was not a chore for Linda, but something she looked forward to and something that made her feel young and healthy.

For years, Wednesday was the day Linda and Bev met for lunch. Another great part of the weekly schedule that made working full-time seem easier. It was their version of "hump day" and once they had lunch and caught up on news to stay in touch with what was going on in each other's lives, the week was already half over. Bev had lived only 12 minutes away so for 40 years they were lucky to be able to enjoy lunch in person – what a treat. Now, since Bev lived in Florida, they settled for virtual lunches. With the new technology available, it was almost as good.

The big screen "portal" that each of them had installed made them appear actual size.

"Alexa, call Bev", Linda prompted the ubiquitous smart home portal. "If you can't be there, feel there" the ads claimed. At times, Linda wondered if they were somehow fooling themselves into believing that they were still as in touch as their used to be before Bev and Harry retired. "Feels like being together in the same room even when you're far apart". Well, Linda had to admit it did feel like they were together... most of the time. As for the privacy of their conversations, well, Linda and Bev had waited several years before jumping on the bandwagon with Portal. This was the typical approach Linda had practiced from working in healthcare IT. Let someone else to test out the shiny new objects and uncover the flaws and experience the unintended consequences – or maybe even in this case, the intentional spying on people in their own homes. Oh well, as long as you were talking about mundane issues it really didn't matter. But Linda still only trusted Alexa at no more than 80 percent.

Bev's face popped up on the screen along with a background of blue sky, palm trees and golf course fairway. "Did you get my text this morning?" she asked.

"No, I have been heads down grading my capstone papers this morning and have not looked at my phone", Linda replied.

"I heard from the travel agent and we need to get our final payment in by Friday to lock in our spot." Bev rummaged through her emails to verify the date.

"Okay, I'll make sure I send it in today. We decided to upgrade to a top deck room with a private balcony to fully enjoy the views. Only 89 days until we leave."

This year they had decided to celebrate and go on a cruise down the Danube River. A group of 14 had been formed with some people from Chicago and some from Florida. Ten days to travel, relax and explore ... together - face-to-face. "What else is going on?" Linda prompted.

"Well, the kids will be visiting next week. I'm looking forward to seeing little Scotty. He's going to be four on Thursday. He is doing well; they are all doing well."

"So hard to believe it is already four years," Linda murmured.

"Our climate change group is planning a Care for Nature lecture and discussion about the impact of global warming on Florida. There will be an expert guest speaker from the Everglades National Park. Did you know it is the third largest national park in the lower 48 states? Last month the group had taken an alligator airboat tour. Some people even held a baby alligator." Thinking back, Bev said, "I thought the best part was seeing the manatee. With all the parks Harry and I visited over the years, we never got to Everglades.

"Next time I visit we should plan to go bird watching again. I read there have been 300 bird species sighted. I still want to see a Painted Bunting and a Bald Eagle. This time we can go down to Edo Pond".

"You know I'm always up for that", said Bev. "What is going on at the university this week?"

"Tuesday is our last faculty meeting for the year. It's already coming up on the end of the semester, with commencement next week. This year I spoke at the annual career day. It starts at 4:30, my part will happen at 5:30 so I will leave after that. Still it gets me home late – I should be back by 8:00 or so. I enjoy my work, but I dread late nights and long days like this. It is a safety concern to be on campus at that hour. This year I rearranged my schedule to work from home the next day so that will help. It sounds minor, but I just don't bounce back like I used to."

"What are you and David doing this weekend?" Bev inquired.

"We will go up to the lake house. We have tickets to a jazz concert over at Williams Bay College on Saturday. I'm looking forward to that. We will probably spend time out on the dock reading. Wilson loves to swim in the lake and then lay in the warm sun. We'll have a picnic lunch. Remember how much Tasha and Cal enjoyed swimming at your house? We had some beautiful summer days out on the dock with the cool breeze. Have you ever thought about coming back up here to spend the summers? You could come from June through October and enjoy the best of Chicago weather. You know our guest house is always open to you. It gives everyone some privacy, yet we can enjoy some regular time together. Would you want to come for a couple of weeks and see what you think?"

The guest house was a new feature at Linda and David's lake house. Not too far from the university, it was their dream after 35 years of living in the congested and expensive northwest suburbs of Chicago. Linda had studied the pros and cons of moving to a condo – the homeowners association costs were too risky - a blank check for the association to do whatever they wanted. Instead, David and Linda had bought a modest three-bedroom ranch on two acres and had built a 600 square foot guest house on the property.

It was cozy with a wood burning stove and an open living space with a kitchenette and large windows that gave a view of the woods and lake. A screened in front porch and bluestone patio added 300 square feet more living space. When nobody was staying with them, Linda used the guest cottage as a studio for various projects. A few times they had rented the space for a few months to a student. It was always available for family or friends who were visiting or who needed a space while they were transitioning their living situation.

"I will be sure to visit – maybe early fall. I could plan on coming for a month to enjoy the changing colors," Bev mused while she munched her watermelon salad. "In the meantime, we have our trip to look forward to. I have started to think about whether I will stay down here now that Harry is gone. It's not the same and I may decide to rent out this place and make Chicago my permanent residence again."

"That would be fantastic, just like old times. You could still get away for the winter – maybe even rent a place near where you are now. What do most people at Leisure Falls do in the summer? How many are year-rounders?" Linda asked.

Linda couldn't imagine living in Florida for the summer or putting up with hurricane season each year. She loved the midwest's seasons and beautiful summers, but she had to admit, escaping for a few weeks during the winter would be the perfect answer.

"Well, I better get back to work. I have a call at 1:00 today with one of my students." Linda said as she finished the last bite of her turkey and avocado sandwich. "I'll talk with you over the weekend sometime. I'll be interested to hear more of your thinking on coming up north." That would be another big change, but if you think you are ready to do it, David and I will help any way we can."

"Ok, talk with you in a couple of days."

They both signed off. Linda got up and wandered to the back door to gaze at her garden. She never got tired of this view. It would be so nice to have Bev back in Chicago. She decided to allow herself a 10-minute walk around the block with Wilson. They headed out the door and down the lawn.

"Much better lunch call", Bev thought as she hung up the phone. "A trip to pack for!" She hadn't felt this energized in a long time...well two and a half years to be accurate. Harry had always teased her that nothing made her happier than planning for a vacation trip. They had been fortunate enough to travel extensively, mostly to Europe. Plus, all those long-ago camping trips with the kids to national parks and Cape Hatteras. This would be her first adventure without Harry, she realized. She fought the urge to call Linda back, begging off, but remembered her vow of last week to re-engage. She knew Ruthie would approve of a week-long cruise down the Danube.

Ruthie, now 31, had inherited her mom's travel bug and had been able to infect her husband Ken. They were young 30-somethings with good jobs and no plans yet to have kids. Although they led busy lives up in Chicago's Lincoln Park, Ruthie and Ken always planned a grand adventure in August, their anniversary month. Ross, her oldest at 34 and his wife Debbie, were expecting their second child early next year and Scotty was excited to be a big brother. He usually spent most of his thrice weekly calls to Granny explaining in elaborate detail how the nursery was being set up and how all the electronic baby gadgets worked. It seemed a forgone conclusion that his attention to detail would segue into a career in engineering like his dad and Grandpa Harry. How Harry would have loved to debate the pros and cons of various baby monitors with little Scotty. He was missing so much!

Bev's giddy enthusiasm over the upcoming trip threatened to disintegrate. She angrily wiped away a few tears and resolutely turned her thoughts to her youngest child Jason. Jason had been an unexpected birthday gift at 40, the best surprise of her life she often said. He was gentle and kind and probably smarter than all of them put together. At 22, just out of college, (engineering of course) he was just starting his life. Following his big sister into city life, he had an apartment in Roscoe Village, close to Ruthie. Ross and Debbie on the other hand, had moved to the Chicago suburbs, tired of the crowded neighborhoods and lack of convenient parking. How in the world did she get stuck all alone at the southern tip of the country, isolated from her kids, her best friend Linda and even her more liberal political beliefs? She decided there and then that a life 1200 miles away from all that she loved was ridiculous. She resolved to talk to Linda about moving back north while on the river cruise. Perhaps during her fall visit to Linda's guest house, they could do some house hunting together. Wow, an upcoming trip and a probable move back north---things were looking up.

It was ironic how slowly Bev had made any real attachments in Leisure Falls, considering how ostentatiously friendly everybody was, not to mention the myriad of available activities. The choices of clubs, classes and lectures was overwhelming with golf being the raison d'etre for most of the men and quite a few of the gals. Bev had enjoyed golf up north. In fact, her life in the Chicago burbs had been filled to the brim with lots of outdoor stuff packed into those short but oh so sweet northern summers.

Bev had always been fairly extroverted. Besides Linda, she had a whole tribe of close women friends in Illinois. But in Florida, while she enjoyed the company of the gals in her golf league, she hadn't made a close friend. Well except for Edna. Edna, even in her mid-seventies, was a force to be reckoned with. Tall, rangy with long grey hair down to her waist, Edna was a true remnant from the hippy era. She had fierce opinions on almost everything and had participated in hundreds of marches back in the 60's. Even in her golden years, Edna kept up with current politics. She was vehement in her criticism of the current administration and was constantly calling the state legislature to complain. Edna had even participated in the Women's March in DC last summer, although the excursion had been too much for her physically and she had returned to Florida exhausted.

That trip, likely the last march of her life, seemed to age her and had left her at times a bit confused. Not quite dementia, but not her old sharp self either. Sometimes in the middle of a discussion over the latest outrageous presidential tweets, Edna would fade into the past. But Bev didn't mind---she found Edna's exploits back in the 60's fascinating. Edna firmly believed that Americans had an obligation to rally against beliefs they felt were contrary to the ideals of the founding fathers. Their patriotic duty was to fight injustices, and like the revolutionaries of 1776, this sometimes involved a little civil disobedience.

Edna's latest crusade had to do with next week's July 4 celebration at Leisure Falls. In the past, all holiday events were free and open to all residents and guests. This year, however, the board had decided that a special VIP section would be offered. For $50 residents could enjoy reserved seats close to the parade and an air-conditioned tent with beer, wine and soft drinks included. Edna, and many other residents, were outraged. They considered this elitism and definitely not compatible with a community spirit. Just maybe, Bev mused, this outrage was the first chink in Leisure Falls Republican-bent armor. A two-tiered system of the haves and have-nots was never a positive outcome, even over something as inconsequential as an Independence Day celebration at a retirement community in central Florida. A small rift but never-the-less a definite awareness of inequity in an otherwise homogenous community of upper middle-class white Americans.

Ready to run some errands, Bev grabbed her keys—not to an SUV or a Prius liked Linda drove up north. No, these stubby keys fit the ignition to her golf cart, painted a royal blue festooned with yellow daisy chains. In LF, everyone drove golf carts and not the drab white or black ones used on the golf courses up north. Here, golf carts were extremely personalized, a creative expression of one's personality. She started her cart up and puttered off

Chapter 5 – August 2019[2]

What a great idea it had been to upgrade their flight to Budapest, Linda congratulated herself. Yes, it had cost more, but it was completely worth it to be able to fully recline and get some sleep before starting the river cruise. The other Lufthansa amenities such as champagne, a red velvet Oreo trifle and a warm neck roll were just the thing for making the 9-hour flight more relaxing. David was engrossed in reading the latest spy thriller on his Kindle. Every now and then his head would bob as he drifted off for a moment. Linda looked over at Bev who was also reading. Everyone was doing their best to enjoy or endure the flight. The excitement of taking their long-awaited river cruise was gradually building as they finally reached the last two hours of the flight.

When they arrived at Terminal 2B at Budapest Ferenc Liszt International Airport, they were greeted by a young woman named Anja dressed in a red suit and holding a sign with the name of the cruise line. All the passengers gathered around her as she ticked off the names on her list to ensure that everyone was accounted for. All baggage received a red sticker with the name of the cruise line. Finally, Anja held up her sign and spoke to the group, "We are leaving from door number 5. Our bus is waiting there to take you to the ship. Please follow me to door number 5." Anja steadily walked through the crowd with the red sign bobbing reassuringly above her head, visible to all the travelers in her group. They

---

[2] https://www.theatlantic.com/ideas/archive/2020/06/american-orbanism/612658/

fell into line and gradually processed to door number 5 and boarded the bus. Thirty minutes later they arrived at Viking Pier and boarded the VIKING VILHJALM and checked in to staterooms #206 and #208.

"We planned to meet everyone at the ship's bar for introductions and then move on to lunch on the deck", Linda reminded David and Bev. "I am looking forward to meeting the rest of the group from Florida. ". The rest of the day was spent getting to know the others in the group and seeing the sights of Budapest. Although there were links between everyone in the group, this was the first time they all had met face-to-face. From Bev's former business partner and member of Bev and Linda's book club, Karen along with her husband Tim were also on the cruise. Several couples had worked with Tim for years in the insurance business and now had retired to Florida. Karen's best friend Lori had come with her brother from Colorado.

Although the group came from diverse parts of the country, there were many similarities among them in terms of age (all nearing or just beginning retirement), interests - such as commitment to an active and healthy lifestyle. Although they were all part of the so called "baby boomer" generation, they were noticeably different from older boomers. The Internet and cell phones were technologies invented within their lifetime and this group had all adopted these new tools and devices for work and were active on social media. The recent presidential election had led to all having mixed feelings about what they were seeing on social media. News reports about the interference of the Russians in the last presidential election were shocking and cause for serious concern for the upcoming election. Never before had politics been such a big part of everyday life and it was both informative and draining to have these serious news reports 24/7.

Sergie, their tour guide for the day, provided excellent information on the history of Budapest and interspersed stories of his personal experiences during the Nazi and communist takeovers of Hungary. His personal opinions were carefully concealed but subtle clues and the words and phrases he used, such as "propaganda" or 'puppets" and the country being given up "free of charge" provided insight to how it felt to have civil rights and freedoms taken away. "Everything the communists touched was spoiled", Sergie remembered. "It was impossible to travel freely. My mother was not able to attend her brother's funeral even though it was only a few miles over the Austrian border. When the wall came down in 1989, it was like coming into a wonderland. There were kind people, goods were plentiful and no limits or long lines to get it. Our lives improved very much after the fall of communism. Higher quality, lower prices and freedoms we had not experienced for 40 years."

Linda reflected on the current situation in the US and the slow but steady drip of changes in many areas by the current administration in Washington. Recently, the president had begun to form a new government media outlet because "the media gives me terrible coverage and reports nothing but fake news". It certainly did not add up to the kinds of changes seen by these people in Europe who had lived through communism, but it was very disturbing none-the-less.

After hours of sightseeing, the tour left the Hungarian Parliament to relax at a nearby old-fashioned restaurant – Hungarikum Bisztro. They ordered chicken crepes and goulash soup for starters followed by crispy duck leg with braised cabbage and onion mash and pork tenderloin dishes made from old family recipes. Dinner was accompanied by live music, and the evening ended with cinnamon apple pie with vanilla sauce.

At the end of the meal, the bill came, along with a shot of plum palinka, a traditional fruit brandy in Central Europe. As Dori the server brought the palinka, the proprietor explained that "Pálinka should be served at 18–23 °C (64–73 °F) because it is at this temperature that the fine smell and taste of the fruit can be best enjoyed. If served too cold, the smell and the taste will be difficult to appreciate."

She went on to inform them that the form of the glass used to drink pálinka affects the drinking experience. The ideal glass is wide at the bottom and narrow at the rim, so that it is tulip shaped. The narrow neck of the glass concentrates the "nose" released from the larger surface at the bottom of the glass, magnifying the smell of the drink."

"To a memorable trip with great friends," Bev toasted. They all raised their glasses and soaked in the delicious atmosphere. After returning to the ship, some of the group gathered again in the bar for a nightcap. Bev, Karen, Lori and Linda gathered around a small table and enjoyed a digestif ruby port as they wound down from the first day of their trip.

"It wasn't on my list of must-see destinations, but I have to say, Budapest is a lovely city." Karen said. "I feel safe walking around and the view of the two sides along the river is spectacular."

"Yes, I can see why they call it "the Paris of the East". However, I also sense an undercurrent of political unrest. Nothing you can see on the surface and in the tourist areas, but when you read the news, they have some serious issues with the politics of Prime Minister Viktor Orban." Linda pointed out.

"He is provoking lots of controversy with his views on immigration and I read his recent meeting with Driscoll is expected to help him in upcoming elections." said Lori.

"The parallels between Oban and Driscoll are remarkable," Karen mused. "While both men lead what are ostensibly democracies, they are each promoting a national distrust of international institutions, opposition to immigration and independent media. In my opinion, it's more of an autocracy."

"They say traveling helps to get a broader perspective. You see and hear much more than we do back in the states. The media really does influence what we hear and decide what is news. That is why I like to read the BBC and other news directly. I am sure we will learn a few surprising things on this trip," said Bev.

"No doubt the US does not hold a corner on the market for crazy politics and biased media. When you see authoritarianism creeping in you see how insidious it is – how it can happen right under your nose if you are not paying attention," Linda added.

Linda seemed deep in thought. Bev could almost see the wheels turning inside Linda's head. She recognized that look- it usually meant that some plan was brewing.

"Yes, or even with some groups cheering it on. How different people can look at the same information and come up with opposite interpretations of it is hard to understand," said Lori.

"I for one, will be looking at what happens with these elections. I want to see how well these other versions of democracy actually work," said Karen.

Bev took the last sip from her glass and declared that her evening was finally at an end. "I am looking forward to relaxing on the bed with the sliding door open to watch the Danube drift by my window." They all agreed, said goodnight and made their way back to their cabins anticipating another exciting day ahead.

Chapter 6- August 2019

The next day of the trip was just as wonderful. After a visit to the Buda Castle, they walked along the river and saw the chilling Shoes on the Danube Bank memorial, a series of 60 pairs of steel sculpted shoes commemorating Jews shot here by the Nazis.

At the end of the day, Bev plopped herself into the oversized club chair. She rubbed her sore feet, glancing around the dimly lit bar located on the upper level of the Viking river boat. While she waited for Linda, David and the rest of the vacation gang to join her for a nightcap, she thought over all the events of that endlessly long day. It was hard to believe that just two nights ago she'd slept in a bed half a world away. She was weary but also excited and even happyish. Travel had always made her excited and happy, so much so that she often slept very little on trips. She remembered all those nights in European hotels with Harry, listening to his heavy night breathing and occasional snores while she lay there buzzing with energy.

In Norway, she had sat out on the balcony till 3 am, just breathing in the beauty of the fjords under a deep rosy sky. Well tonight it would just be her, alone in her cabin, so cunningly arranged with hidden storage everywhere and that amazing river view. She could watch the river all night without worrying that she might be disturbing Harry's sleep. A couple of gin tonics might be needed for that vision of solitude to seem more inviting. She searched the bar for signs of Linda and was rewarded with a grin as Linda waved and David carried a tray with Bev's gin tonic, a prosecco for Linda and David's Guinness. Soon the bar was filled with lively conversation as the rest of the group filtered in, grabbed drinks and sat down, the fourteen of them eager to rehash their day in Budapest and anticipate the week's cruise down the Danube through Austria and into Germany.

"Hey Bev, you look great" Linda whispered. "That haircut is cute, and I love that blouse". Bev blushed with pleasure over Linda's compliments. Guess the big effort to pull herself together had paid off. Ruthie had flown down to Florida for a few days just before the trip and had led her mom through a marathon of shopping and salon treatments...exhausting but fun, and, judging from Linda's admiring looks, worth every penny.

Bev's thoughts were interrupted by a booming male voice extolling" It's everywhere! Here in Hungary, Great Britain, the Philippines and now in our own country. Nationalism, Populism, Isolationism---all the same thing. An excuse to put greed and self-interest above the greater good. A way of dividing our country and even the world into us vs. them ". By now most of the bar's attention was centered on Tim. Like most of their group, Tim was appalled at the policies of Driscoll and Co. and the almost daily racist and misogynistic tweets from the President.

Tim continued his rant," The man's a bully and has no-"

A tall well-dressed man sitting at the bar interrupted." That's all well and good but my 401K is in great shape, unemployment is at a new low, and Driscoll isn't taking any shit from anyone. He's standing up for America, instead of rolling over like that last guy, who made us look weak. You liberals are soft. We finally have a real patriot in the oval office. "

Tim started to reply but his wife Karen squeezed his arm, reminding him that a luxury river cruise was not an appropriate political venue. The two men glared at each other, finally turning their attention back to their drinks. Bev sighed in relief that the argument wasn't escalating. Passengers on a cruise like this were usually well- to- do, well-educated and well-traveled. These ships saw very few bar room brawls but partisan tensions ran high these days where American politics were concerned.

Everyone in Bev's group was anxious to diffuse the awkwardness and talk soon turned to the next day's excursions in Budapest as well as everyone's past travels to Europe. Lori, the group's foodie and an experienced European traveler, remarked "My favorite part of these trips is the food. It seems as if every little café and hole in the wall restaurant takes pride in their homemade dishes, most from old family recipes. No processed food like we see everywhere in the states. And don't get me started on the bread here", she groaned.

Linda added," But what impresses me is that work life, leisure and family time seem more balanced. Americans seem like hamsters running on their treadmills, endlessly working but getting nowhere. And the suburban sprawl of chain restaurants, huge discount stores and concrete and cement everywhere really gets me down. How many Walgreens does one town need? How many grocery stores? That's what spurred us to move north to Wisconsin. It's close to our friends and family in the Chicago area but the pace of life seems more reasonable. "

"And the golf fees are much cheaper" added David with a smile.

At that point, most of the group started leaving the bar for their cabins. Tomorrow's tour of Hero's Square and the Museum of Fine Arts left at 8:30 am and no one wanted to oversleep and miss the sumptuous breakfast buffet. Bev found herself for the first time all day alone with Linda and David as the bar slowly emptied.

"Bev, everything OK? "David asked. David was perhaps the kindest man Bev knew. He and Linda had been married for over 30 years and up until their recent move to Wisconsin, they lived in a town near to where she and Harry had lived all their married life. Not having had children, Linda and David were especially close, sharing a full life together that included busy careers, golf, travel and a series of beloved golden retrievers. When Harry had died of a sudden heart attack, they had dropped everything, staying with Bev for a month while she learned how to process her overwhelming grief and begin a life alone. David had helped with the more practical issues... the finances, house upkeep etc. Bev had left all that to Harry and was embarrassed to discover how little she knew of those matters. Linda had been her emotional rock, patiently listening for hour after hour as Bev cycled between rage and abject sorrow. Slowly, Bev had come to terms with her new reality.

Under David's tutelage, she had organized all her finances and had undergone a crash course in home and car maintenance. Now, more than two years later, she felt for the most part in control. And LF had plenty of handymen for all those tasks she wasn't up to.

Bev started to reply that she was fine, just bone tired, when 2 couples approached from the other side of the lounge. Like most of the

Viking passengers, they were well dressed and appeared to be in their upper sixties.

"Sorry to barge in. My name's Rodger and this here is my wife Cathy and our mates Lew and Carol. Being from Sydney, this is our first cruise with primarily Americans, and we couldn't help but be curious about that little spat earlier. "

David invited them to sit and soon a fresh round of drinks arrived.

"How do Australians view the political scene in the US?" asked Linda.

"Well we had a real hard time understanding how your President Driscoll got elected in the first place---wasn't he on one those reality shows? He's not a government guy, right? We all thought that gal Hillary had it locked up. What the heck happened?"

"Most of us are still trying to figure that one out" David replied wryly. Everyone chuckled at that.

"Well at least you'll be getting rid of him next year. "

"Maybe not" David replied. "That man who spoke up had a point. Many Americans have been doing well over the last 2 years and I'm worried that there are too few Republicans that will change their vote in 2020. They may disagree and even despise the man but if their bank accounts are healthy, they seem able to overlook his ridiculous comments and discriminatory policies. The huge issues like gun control, health care and climate change don't seem to garner enough outrage to tip the scales. While these issues effect all American citizens, they've been labeled as liberal democratic concerns and are not getting the proper attention in Congress. I think it's a very real possibility that barring an enormous snafu, Driscoll will be reelected. "

"I think a key factor will be the voter turn-out," Linda spoke up. "Last time, only 43% of eligible voters actually voted. Major blocks such as minorities and younger voters did not turn out as they did with Obama. These groups are being negatively impacted by Driscoll policies, so they need to get out to vote this time. I also think the healthcare issue has become a much bigger factor. Since Obamacare passed, there has been a huge shift in consumer literacy on healthcare. People know what a pre-existing condition is now, and they realize their vulnerability if there is no coverage. People also have been experiencing the rising costs of healthcare – it has gotten worse than ever in the past 3 years. Special interests such as pharmaceutical companies and hospitals are charging astronomical prices that nobody can pay – even if they do have insurance coverage. "

"I read an article last week that the majority of American could not cover an unexpected health expense of $400! You really can't get any kind of healthcare for $400. I recently had 5 stitches removed – a 10-minute visit – and was charged $275 for that office visit. My insurance paid none of it since I have not met my deductible yet this year. I guess it is good not to meet your deductible since it means you are healthy, but you can see where people will avoid going to the doctor if it means bills they cannot pay. Don't even get me started on the cost of a colonoscopy!"

"To me, this is the biggest issue facing us and I now have zero confidence that either party will fix it before we get to Medicare. In fact, some of the politicians want to decrease Medicare benefits. It is all enough to make you want to move out of the country – anywhere else in the world, healthcare expenses don't bankrupt people, people have access to the care they need and they don't worry about it all the time like we Americans do. It is truly a dystopian nightmare; we're all hoping with our fingers crossed that nothing bad happens with our health. It's no way to live."

The Australians shook their heads and said they sympathized with Americans on the healthcare issue and could not understand why this problem could not be solved as it has been for all other countries.

Linda said, "It's all about the special interests. They run the country now; our democracy is corrupted and morally bankrupt. The almighty dollar is the deciding factor for everything. It is so discouraging. This is why we intend to enjoy ourselves on this trip and not check email or news for 10 days. We all need a break from this negativity. "

On that sobering and dismal note, Bev left for her cabin. She wondered what kind of disruption could possibly prevent Driscoll's reelection if none of his past indiscretions, inappropriate remarks and divisive policies had convinced his supporters that he was not acting in the county's best interest.

Later in the week the cruise offered an optional excursion to the Vienna Opera House. The Wiener Staatsoper is one of the leading opera houses in the world steeped in tradition. It officially opened on May 25, 1869, with Mozart's DON JUAN – attended by the Emperor Franz Joseph and Empress Elisabeth. As they entered the opera house, Linda and Bev read information about its history. "Over 350 performances are given each year featuring more than 60 different operas and ballets. After being bombed in 1945 during WWII, the opera house was restored and reopened on November 5, 1955." The performance that night was Beethoven's *Fidelio* and the opening ceremonies were broadcast by Austrian television.

The significance of the opera house was its extraordinary celebration of music, but more than that, full restoration of the opera house symbolized and celebrated artistic freedom which had been forbidden during the Nazi period. When it finally reopened, the whole world understood that life was beginning again for Austria and that democracy and freedom came with their new independence.

Today, the Vienna State Opera is considered one of the most important opera houses in the world, because it has the largest repertoire. Tonight, they would be seeing the opera *Mannon* by Jules Massenet. They had arrived early so spent some time exploring and then finally found their seats to enjoy the performance.

At one time earlier in their marriage, Linda and David had owned a coffeehouse in downtown Evanston, Illinois named The Opera Café.

Sandwiches, pasta, and desserts were available along with specially brewed coffee. The real reason people came to the opera café was to hear the live opera music performed several times throughout the evening by the waitstaff who were music performance majors at nearby Northwestern University. During this period, Linda learned many of the famous arias from Mozart, Verdi and Puccini operas to accompany the singers. David, who had no musical background, worked full-time in the café and ended up learning quite a bit about opera from listening to it all day. His favorite was the emotional and dramatic Nessun Dorma, Puccini's aria from the opera *Turandot*, which includes the lyrics: "None shall sleep, even you, oh Princess, in your cold room", "watch the stars that tremble with love and hope, no one will know his name and we must, alas, die"." Attending the opera this evening was nostalgic and brought back memories of those earlier days in their marriage when they dove into a new venture and made a dream of their come true.

On the next day, the ship traveled to Linz. The day of touring had been exhausting but exhilarating. As passengers finished dinner, some drifted upstairs into the lounge for a night-cap and to enjoy the stories of the day. Their group gathered by the bar and Linda and Bev reviewed pictures from the Austrian countryside. It was so beautiful with small villages with two or three cafes and stores. There were no massive malls with acres of parking and no rows off strip-mall retail stores that offered no charm and were not within walking distance of anyplace. In these Austrian villages, there was almost little traffic and a pace much slower than the one in the northwest Chicago suburbs. The food was obviously fresh and local and there was certainly no such thing as Walmart and Big Box stores.

Linda reported, "The food processing industry in Austria only has to provide for 8.3 million people compared to 330 million in the U.S. I read that the most important products are brewing, non-alcoholic beverages, confectionary, meat and fruit juice. Austria has one of the highest standards of living in Europe and it certainly shows. It is amazing that only 27,000 people work in the Austrian food processing sector. The traditional Austrian diet is based on pork, flour, and vegetables and there is an increasing interest in healthy lifestyles - similar to what we hear people talking about in the US."

From what they had seen today, the lifestyle looked very healthy with lots of walking, many low sugar food options and enjoyment of other things altogether such as music and art. It was also clear that Austrians are very environmentally aware and valued food products that are sustainably produced. Linda had also read that biotech food products have a negative image overall and the market for organic accounts for 5% in in retail food and Austria has the highest percentage of organic farms in the EU. This compares equally with the US – once we get going on an idea it can really take off. Not only are organic food options now at 5% in the US, they accounted for over $50 billion!

These issues were important to Linda and David. It seemed to be an uphill battle in the US, but here the atmosphere was different and there seemed to be a genuine interest in doing the right things and providing healthy choices. Was this just an idyllic vacation view or was there really something to this? Living in the US seemed great for many people, but it was also not great for an increasing number who not only did not eat healthy food, 1 in 8 had food insecurity and were at risk for hunger. It did not seem that the Congress could solve any problem – or even make some progress. Was it easier with a smaller country or was there really something decaying and corrupt going on in the US?

David sat with the men having a final diet coke for the day. On their last cruise, Linda and David rang up a whopping $32 bar bill for the week – mostly diet cokes. Linda drifted over to a group where Bev sat and the ladies were animatedly comparing notes on the adventures of the day. Bev was showing everyone her new leather purse. She was famous for buying new bags on her travels around the world.

"Has anyone seen this article?" Linda asked. "Catchy headline - Sounds like Austria has their political problems too. It seems to be everywhere."

"Trump in a slim-fit suit"

On May 17, German media released a secret video showing the head of Austria's far-right Freedom Party — which was a core part of Kurz's ruling coalition — trying to collude with a supposed Russian national to influence the 2017 Austrian elections.

"I am still here," Kurz told supporters at a rally three hours after the no-confidence vote. "They cannot stop the change we have started," he boomed as chants of "Chancellor Kurz!" rang out from the crowd. Kurz also took tough stands on immigration himself during the election campaign and while in power, especially against asylum seekers hoping to enter Europe. Those positions, among others, led critics to call him "Trump in a slim-fit suit."

Alex Ward, Vox.com, May 28, 2019

"Same tune, different orchestra, sounds very familiar," Karen said, raising her eyebrows to invite further comments from the group.

"I'm seeing a pattern, but it remains to be seen how people in the different countries will respond to it. Everywhere we go, there is still a strong effort to remember the destruction brought by the Nazi's the last time they let nationalism get out of control," Lori said.

"Yes, all of the tour guides mention the influence of fascism, how it rose, and they even share how it affected them personally. It's almost like they are sending us a message. They never fail to emphasize the work they have done, not to eliminate it from society, but to purposely build in ways to remember that awful time as a way to never let it happen again." Karen gazed out the window as she reflected on her experiences, which they all agreed were part of what was so memorable about the touring.

"Apparently it will take more than just remembering, there is already backsliding towards a repeat of nationalism building into something even more damaging," Linda said. "We are in the same position now, although we were on the right side of history last time. It is no guarantee that we will always be on the right side."

The conversation drifted into anticipation of the next day of the trip. Linda decided to put the news aside; it never did her any good to read news after dinner if she wanted to get a good night's sleep. She looked over at David enjoying himself as he always did in social situations, this is where he really felt at home. She enjoyed herself too, but at the end of a busy day like this she was exhausted so she sat back to relax, listen to the other's laughter and tried to push it all into a small corner at the back of her mind.

Bev contentedly patted her new handbag. Of course, another purse was not something she needed but the beautiful turquoise color had called to her from the recesses of the little Viennese shop – she was such a sucker for blue in any shade. She noticed that the boat had picked up speed, carrying them smoothly westward towards Krems. She was tempted to call it a night and retire to her room, probably with one or two of those insanely delicious chocolate macadamia nut cookies, too conveniently available at the coffee and tea station. However, she was hoping for a few minutes alone with Linda.

After spending several days with the lively traveling group, her life in Florida seemed even more isolated and lonely. She was determined to act on her decision to move north. Bev was confident that she would have no trouble renting her home in Leisure Falls – there was a steady stream of northerners anxious to explore their retirement options and many wanted to rent before purchasing. Bev knew Linda would applaud her plan to come back to Chicago and she would most likely have some helpful suggestions as to where to begin looking. Bev had always felt that Linda was the smartest person she knew. That fierce intelligence combined with a natural reserve could make Linda seem intimidating to those that didn't know her well, but that sometimes formidable exterior hid an empathy and compassion that was second to none. Linda could be counted on unequivocally to come to the aid of her close friends as Bev could only too well attest. While Bev often got sidetracked by the tangential aspects of an issue, Linda was able to zero in on the crux of the matter and contribute ideas that were both creative and based in common sense.

Bev felt an urgent need to share her decision with Linda as if declaring it aloud would be a first tangible step to making it happen. She was suddenly ready to outwait the others all night if need be. Slowly they all left for bed, Linda miraculously remaining as if she had intuited that Bev needed to speak with her privately.

"Linda", Bev began. "I've made the decision to move back North. I need your advice as to how to get started. I am hoping we can find something when I visit in the fall…nothing fancy…maybe just a rental…I would really like to be settled in before Christmas. Wouldn't it be great if I could spend the holidays with the kids and hopefully with you and David?" Bev's words started to tumble out as she became more and more excited at the prospect of a northern holiday season in a place of her own. As she stopped to catch her breath, Linda put a gentle hand on her shoulder.

"Bev", Linda spoke quietly but with measured intent and gravity. "That's great and of course I'll help, David will too, but…" and here she paused before finishing her sentence with an assignment that would change a great many things in their lives for the next year "…but first there is unfinished business in Florida…for you and I both" Linda went on to explain, leaning in closely, keeping a steadying hand on Bev's shoulder. And they talked and conspired late into the night under a warm Austrian sky.

Bev woke the next morning, her mouth dry and her brain muzzy as if she had indulged in too many gin tonics although she hadn't even had one. As she gradually came back into herself, she played back all the words that she and Linda had spoken…words that had coalesced into half-formed plans as the boat had glided down the wide placid river. The idea that Linda had proposed had at first seemed preposterous – like something from a New York Times best-selling thriller. After hours of debating, persuading and cajoling, Bev had finally agreed to an audacious idea. She agreed to temporarily postpone her plans to move north so that she could take part in…nothing less than helping to change the course of American history.

As ludicrous as that sounded, Linda's proposal boiled down to that – affect the presidential election by swinging the Florida vote from Republican to Democratic. And accomplish this by making sure that the Republican voting block from Leisure Falls would not be counted. And here is where the plan seemed to veer into the completely nonsensical –keep the population of Leisure Falls distracted or somehow fooled so that they would miss the hours that the voting polls were open.

Linda had said the idea had first occurred to her from a very unlikely source – President Driscoll himself. He had encouraged the American people to vote – but had used the wrong date – November 28. What would happen, Linda had mused, if things had gotten confused and not everyone voted, especially a solid Republican area like Leisure Falls.

Bev had been very skeptical that any of this could actually happen in real life. How could an entire village of 120,000 be made unaware of the actual time? How could they get the days confused? Linda said that it would take a many-pronged approach and admitted that she didn't have specific details worked out, but she was convinced that it was possible. Bev was also skeptical that even if they could pull it off (a huge if), it might not make a large enough impact. Could it really sway an election that seemed destined to give Driscoll four more years in office? Linda spent the wee hours of the night using all her persuasive abilities that the numbers proved if Leisure Falls did not participate in the election, Florida was likely to give the 29 electoral votes to the Democratic candidate and that a Democratic result in Florida could mean the difference in the national election.

In the end, Bev's trust and loyalty to Linda won out. She would stay in Florida until the election was over. Although largely unconvinced, she would give herself over to this insane plan.

What was it about fall that was so exhilarating? The cool temperatures, the smell of leaves, the multi-colored mums that appeared in every yard? Of course, there was also the renewed interest in cooking and the return to chili, beef stew, and gratin recipes. Tonight, for Bev's arrival, Linda was making one of Bev's favorites –homemade pea soup with ham and vegetables. Tomorrow she was planning a more ambitious feast- penne pasta with roasted butternut squash, pancetta and sage. It would all be finished off with an apple galette with goat cheese, sour cherry and almond topping.

Linda reviewed the menus in her head as she headed over to the guest house to make final preparations for Bev's visit. This time Bev had said she would stay for a month, leaving just before the winter snow might begin. The patio was surrounded by short clumps of ornamental grasses and the tall vertical growth and feathery plumes of Karl Foerster grasses shifting to their fall bronze color. Today was one of those perfect fall days with crisp cool air, but warm sun.

As she entered the large open living space, Linda noticed that the house still smelled clean from her previous efforts to spruce up the place. She had been using this for a studio while they did not have guests so she wanted to make sure her projects were packed away and that Bev would find a fresh and clean place in which to put her own things. The kitchen was small, but open to the living space. There was an island with a dark granite top for casual eating. The white cabinets fit in with the open concept making the space seem just right.

Best of all, there were floor to ceiling doors that offered a panoramic view of the lake. When open, it was like you were camping outdoors, the perfect combination of indoor/outdoor living. Linda often used this space for her writing and had taken up some small painting projects. The effect of nature on her mind allowed the introspection and creativity to flow. In the winter it was just as wonderful to look at the frozen landscape and feel the desolation of outdoors while enjoying the warmth of the fireplace. If she did not have to commute in the winter weather, Linda found it to be very enjoyable – for a while. By the time February ended, she and David were ready for it to be over. When they finally retired, they would take a few of the winter weeks and visit friends and family and take vacations.

Linda checked the ¾ size refrigerator to make sure the grocery delivery had arrived. There were a few essentials: bread from the bakery in town and a few items from the local farmers market to get Bev started. On many of the evenings they would all eat dinner together in the main house. Sometimes Bev would chop vegetables and make the salad while David grilled chicken or skirt steaks. These dinners along with a crock pot of chili or split pea soup would be all they needed.

Since Bev was visiting, the book club meeting would take place at Linda's this month. They had gotten used to virtual attendance by Bev, but this would be a special treat to have a face-to-face book club. This book club had been meeting for almost 20 years. Over that time, they had purposely kept the group small – only 5 members. This group of women had many things in common and by now had gone through many life passages together including new jobs, divorce, heart attacks, deaths of family members, children's marriages and becoming grandparents.

Of course, they all loved reading, and the book club had read over 200 books on many topics. Beyond the discussion of the book, Bev, Linda, Karen, Dawn and Kim had also discussed politics at each meeting. They had weathered the Bush years, relished the Obama years and continued to struggle through the Driscoll years having remarkably similar views on all the issues. After the 2016 election, Linda gave each of the members a book of daily meditations based on the Stoic philosophers. These ideas seemed to be the perfect attitude that would be needed to survive the new administration in Washington DC. Her favorite quote from the meditations was, "Sometimes even to live is an act of courage..." by Seneca.

How many times had this been true when each day seemed to bring a new outrage from Driscoll? Linda wondered how many people who love reading voted for Driscoll in the last election. While there may be some, she suspected that there was a strong correlation between reading and voting democratic.

It was not just the division between Democrats and Republicans though; in the last three years the issues of immigration, gun control and health care seemed to become much more crystallized in terms of what is a reasonable solution that most people want. The biggest issue of all – climate change -was suffering many setbacks with the Driscoll administration reversing air and water regulations, opening up drilling for oil companies in what used to be protected wilderness and just outright disbelief in science and climate change. Recent news showed serious warming trends were melting glaciers. Just this summer the temperature in some Alaskan cities reached into the 80's setting new records. Sometimes it seemed hopeless that we would ever make progress on these serious problems.

As Linda walked out the back door and circled back to the lakefront, Wilson joined her in his usual companionable way. They walked down to the dock where a fire pit surrounded by rocking deck chairs overlooked the lake with a beautiful afternoon sunset. Wilson's relaxed personality always rubbed off on Linda, easing the troublesome thoughts about national and world issues and bringing her back to a simpler focus on the beauty of her personal world and life with David. She reflected on how this was Wilson's whole job in life, and he did it to perfection. We would all be better off if we could just relax like Wilson and "focus on the beautiful things in life" more often.

After sitting and enjoying a few minutes, Linda and Wilson walked back to the main house. David was just pulling in the driveway, coming back from a round of golf. He brought his clubs into the garage and came through the mudroom into the kitchen.

"What time will Bev be arriving?" he asked.

"Her flight gets in at 5:00 so I expect to see her sometime around 6:30 if they are on time," Linda answered.

"Do you feel like making a pizza tonight?"

"Actually, I got the crock pot out today and made split pea soup, which is Bev's favorite. I thought she might be up for a little something to eat when she gets here, but nothing too heavy. Let's plan to make a pizza next week."

Linda's cell phone buzzed. As she picked it up, she saw that Bev was texting that their flight had just landed, and she was headed down to baggage claim. She would be at the lake by 6:30. Linda replied that she had a pot of pea soup ready for her if she were hungry. Bev's reply – "Perfect, just what I have a taste for!". Linda sighed contentedly; this would be a wonderful month.

Chapter 10 – October 2019

"Luck is what happens when preparation meets opportunity."

— Seneca

Bev cruised up Route 50 in her rental car towards Lake Geneva, on a crisp October evening. She had the windows and sunroof open and the heat on high. She had forgotten how fun this combination was – wasteful and frivolous but darn fun. She loved the juxtaposition of a chilly breeze pouring in through the open windows and the comforting heat at her feet, legs and lap. This felt like a harmless guilty pleasure, one that her practical sons would disapprove of. Her back seat contained a crate of honey crisp apples that she had purchased from a Wisconsin roadside stand, as well as a case of David's favorite beer. As much as she felt completely welcome at David and Linda's home, a token of appreciation in the form of Guinness beer might enhance her standing, especially if her visit was extended. Bev felt that the planning needed to pull off this audacious scheme might require more than a few weeks. She might have indulged in some small hope that Linda had cooled on the idea, but knowing her friend's tenacity, it was doubtful indeed.

Before long, Bev pulled up to the house. She always looked forward to visiting Linda's home where she had an entire guest house to herself. Linda and David had planned their retirement home with great care. Years ago, Linda had become interested in small house designs that were cleverly built to maximize living space in less square footage. To create the illusion of spaciousness, they usually incorporated large windows and patios that allowed the outside beauty to become part of the living space. Linda had used beautiful Lake Geneva as her backdrop. Once they had purchased the main house and cultivated the beautiful gardens, they had a smaller guest house built. While compact, the guest house was one of Bev's very favorite places. During her travels with Harry, Bev had always been happy to pay extra for "a room with a view". She had always enjoyed the views offered, ranging from Lake St. Moritz in Switzerland to the Saguaro cacti and Santa Rita mountains of Tucson. And in Bev's opinion, the view of Lake Geneva, Wisconsin from Linda's guest house was just as inspiring. Bev knew that the busy days ahead, full of planning their Florida takeover, would begin and end with that tranquil view.

"Bev, thanks so much for the apples and beer," Linda said, giving Bev a big hug.

"Yes, especially the beer," quipped David. "That will go nicely with the pea soup we're having tonight. Of course, didn't Harry insist that everything goes well with beer?"

Soon Bev, Linda, and David were sitting in the cozy dining room in the main house, enjoying steaming bowls of split pea soup, seven grain bread from the local bakery, and Waldorf salad made from Bev's contribution of locally grown apples. As darkness fell, Bev could hear a few loons on the lake, calling to each other in that eerie cadence. The warm soup, crackling fire in the fireplace and a few glasses of Pinot Noir all contributed to Bev feeling truly contented and relaxed. Tomorrow they would embark on the task at hand but not tonight. Bev would perhaps indulge in a Bailey's and coffee before making her way across the garden to the welcoming flannel sheets of her guest house bed.

The next morning Bev woke at 8:00 AM to a brilliant lapis sky. She enjoyed the dappled autumn light filtering through the leaves, some still green but most crimson and yellow. She heard the click of Wilson's toenails on the blue stone patio outside her window and knew that Linda had most likely been up for several hours. Linda had always enjoyed the early morning hours while Bev tended to lazily fritter those hours away, dozing in her bed or reading from her Kindle. It was especially tempting to loll away a few more minutes when the crisp morning air streaming in from her open window made her want to burrow down even deeper under the down quilt Linda had put on her bed. But the thought of a bracing cup of hot tea and the cherry turnover that Linda had thoughtfully left for her was enough incentive for her to climb out of bed and get dressed.

Linda and Bev spent the day on her patio with a generous pot of coffee and two legal pads. It was difficult to get a handle on just how to begin planning such a large-scale attack on the Florida election process. Bev felt frustrated and inadequate – her knowledge of the IT required to pull this off was nil. By late afternoon they had amassed several pages of ideas but it all still needed to coalesce into a plan. They needed one central idea; some event or scheme that would act as a smoke screen so that LF residents would be otherwise occupied, and Election Day would come and go without their votes. But neither Bev nor Linda could decide on the most feasible solution. By 3:00 PM, they decided to call it a day and take Wilson for a long walk before dinner.

Linda tried to cheer Bev up. "Tomorrow will be better Bev; sometimes ideas just need to percolate."

Bev shrugged and tried to smile but it felt more like a grimace. "Linda, all our ideas so far seem way over my head. I'm not adept at all with this technology stuff like you are. Altering news feeds and doctoring software is a foreign language. Geeze, I still write my columns longhand and beg someone to type it. You picked the wrong person."

Linda could see how miserable her friend was. She gave her a quick hug and steered the conversation away from elections and on to Bev's grandson Scotty. Bev's stomach slowly unclenched as she described Scotty's attempts to fix a leaky bathtub faucet by himself. Soon they were both laughing as Bev ended the anecdote with Scotty sitting in the tub with all of Ross' tools in a pool of rusty water, triumphant that the leak was indeed repaired.

By 9:00 PM Bev was on her way back to the guest house after another great dinner. Linda was a superior cook. Her food was simple, healthy and always delicious and tonight's pasta with butternut squash was no exception. Even after that hearty main course, Bev had managed to polish off two helpings of dessert – a wonderful apple pastry creation that was covered with a cherry and almond topping. Bev had always had a sweet tooth and Linda's delicious desserts were not the time to curb her impulses. Humming to herself, she changed into her nightie and crawled under the covers of her bed. The light from a full moon bathed her room in a golden glow. She felt herself relaxing towards sleep when suddenly her brain clicked on with an idea as bright as the moonlight spilling onto her bed.

Energy surged through her and she bounded up, grabbed a large stack of post-it notes and headed into the living room

*   *   *   *   *

Bev awoke to a light tap on the door. She was curled up on the lounge chair in a room that seemed oddly darkened. She stumbled to the door and opened it to an anxious looking Linda. "Why are all the windows covered?" Linda asked while handing Bev a large mug of coffee. Bev looked around the dim living room. The large windows were completely covered in post-it notes – some in tight groupings, others in a long multi-colored line.

"I had a few ideas" Bev said with a sleepy smile.

"A few!" exclaimed Linda. "It looks like an episode from The Closer in here. OK Brenda Lee Johnson, walk me through it."

Bev walked over to the left window which had the words OPERATION LIFESAVER in bold letters. Below that was about 30 post-it notes. "On the boat you suggested that pulling this off might require many small diversions, but we also need to decide on a main event, something that could include a very large section of Leisure Falls population".

Bev pointed to a timeline. "This event should occur the night before the election. While the participants will think they are attending a 12-hour all-nighter, we will manipulate things so that in reality 24 hours will pass. The event will actually end at 7:00 PM election day when the polls are closed."

Linda broke in, "Which event do you think would work the best at LF?"

Bev pointed to another column of post-it notes "A combination fund-raiser and re-election celebration. And as a special enticement, a series of celebrities along with raffles of big prizes. The best part is, we can hold the entire event in the LF Conference Center. It holds up to 90,000 people and even has a ballroom. That should be plenty since we cannot expect to get everyone living at LF to attend. Last night I googled its availability for Monday November 2 and it's open."

"How should we keep people from knowing the time? There must be hundreds of wall clocks in the conference center plus everyone will have cell phones and watches."

Bev had a quick reply, "We will make everyone turn in their cell phones and watches—entice them to leave the world behind and just enjoy the event. And as for the clocks in the building..." Bev pointed to another post-it list labeled MATT. "Linda, you are very savvy with technology but what we will need is a real IT expert and I was thinking of my brother. Matt is just the guy."

"Bev, I know your brother is a computer genius, but he hasn't left Wisconsin in 30 years. How will he be able to help?"

"Don't worry, I'll reel him in somehow. He's so anti-Driscoll plus I think he will be intrigued by the sheer complexity of our time manipulation problem. I'm sure that adjusting the clocks will be child's play for him. With his computer engineering degree and all his career experience, I know he can handle this. We will also need him for all of the other tech stuff too."

Bev continued outlining her thoughts to Linda, all of which were printed neatly on dozens of post-it notes. She showed Linda the blue post-it which had ideas for the celebrities: singers, news personalities and sports figures. The pink post-its encompassed possible raffle prizes while the green notes covered a list of marketing ideas to promote the event.

"What's on these red post-its?" Linda asked.

Bev paused to take a big gulp of coffee before explaining. "Those are problems that occurred to me that were either too technical for me to consider or just too hard for my tired old brain to solve at 3:00 AM. For instance, that incessant Fox News that's aired over the main square intercoms. For people that don't attend the event, we need to make sure they aren't constantly reminded of getting to the polls that day. I hope Matt can deal with that. Also, I think most Republican voters will find the event exciting and will attend, but what about those Democrats that are especially vocal? Some, like my friend Edna, we may want to enlist, but there are others I am not sure about. The Andersons down the street for example are just loose cannons. I don't trust that they will just sit back and allow the evening to pass without trying to disrupt things."

"It's funny that the biggest threat to our success may come from our fellow Democrats," Linda chuckled, "but I see your point. We have just over a year to plan everything and fix the problems. I'm betting that there will be a lot more yellow post-it notes before we're done."

Linda then suggested that they go into town for a big breakfast to celebrate the breakthrough and continue brainstorming, her treat. Bev happily, although also a bit wearily, agreed and the two drove to town for a morning nosh, all the while chatting excitedly about the upcoming year and all that it would bring.

Chapter 11 – November 2019, one year to go

The sun no longer woke Linda as it did in the summer. Not only was it dark now at 5:30, it was still dark until almost 7:00 am. They were in the dark and cold time of year for Wisconsin. This was not a good time for gardening or golfing, but it was an excellent time for getting other work done indoors. The weather had not turned cold yet, so Linda was still spending some of each day out on the patio watching the lake.

Her thoughts turned to the busy upcoming months and the coming holidays. Linda usually put off thinking about Christmas until late into November. The longer the better. It was exhausting to keep up enthusiasm for all of the holidays for six weeks or more if you let the retail industry have its way. It would be so nice if the holidays came every four years, like the Olympics. Linda considered this every year despite the impossibility of implementing such a plan.

This year, Linda was now focused on implementing their plan. Now that they had laid out the timeline, she could begin to see some of the steps that must be taken. They were shifting from planning mode into action. One thing she had learned in her career was the importance of communications. This project would involve many carefully planned communications and Linda knew that you can never over-communicate on a project – this would be no exception.

It was always helpful to have a documented plan and a picture or visual so the team could easily see at a glance what needed doing. Linda sat down at the computer and pulled up a spreadsheet and started entering some of the key communication events she and Bev had discussed. After an hour she looked back on her work and saw that there were already many more communications needed than they had originally thought. When you start putting things down on paper, you began to get a much clearer picture and inevitably new thoughts come up. As she went through the morning, Linda continued to let the thoughts percolate in her mind. She alternated between doing chores around the house and hurrying back to her computer to put her new inspirations down before she forgot them. She quickly typed in her latest brainstorm – monthly newsletter articles. This would be a placeholder reminding her to fill in details on the topics and craft messages she and Bev would write.

It was Bev's job to get the Board/social committee to approve their idea to hold the fundraiser. This was a perfect assignment for Bev; her natural enthusiasm and bubbling personality were powerful persuasive tools. Few could resist or deny her when she was in full Bev-mode. Linda chuckled to herself at what an unlikely duo they were. Linda prided herself on her calm, deliberate demeaner. She enjoyed a well- ordered life and was disciplined in both her work life and home-being organized made her happy. Bev, on the other hand, was notoriously disorganized. Linda laughed out loud remembering the plethora of post- its that had covered the windows of the guest cottage. But Linda knew, without a doubt in the world, that her life would be flat without her dearest friend, even if she could be exasperating at times.

They would prepare monthly articles for the newsletter to build interest and make sure everyone at LF was talking about it and planning to attend. Linda quickly drafted the content for the November newsletter,

"The Board has approved the proposal to hold a fundraiser event on November 2, 2020 to support LF effort to bring out the vote for the presidential election. This event will be open to all LF residents. "

She stopped and re-read this much. Anything about the election was usually of interest to most of the LF population. Over 90% were registered to vote and they were all attending rallies held by candidates passing through who were already courting the LF vote.

"More details will be provided in upcoming newsletters. Please contact Bev Anderson directly with any questions."

That was probably enough to get some people talking and asking questions. Bev would have to be ready with answers and to collect "input" or suggestions that were bound to be offered. They had agreed that the approach they would take to build a positive attitude for the fundraiser was to accept any and all suggestions for consideration – you never know when someone might have a really good idea that they had not thought of. The fundraiser committee would review all suggestions to make sure everyone felt that they had a chance to give their input.

After spending a couple of hours on this, Linda spent the rest of the afternoon enjoying reading for her book club later that month. Later, after David arrived home, they took Wilson and headed out for a walk by the lake. The sun was still out – rare for November which was usually the gloomiest month of the year. They headed down the path enjoying the crisp air and the setting sun.

David asked, "Is everything proceeding according to plan?"

"Yes, so far it has been full steam ahead. Bev is doing a great job down there. She has a knack for creating a positive energy about things when people first hear about it. She assumes everyone will be as excited about it as she is and talks about how much fun it will be so many of them are reacting positively."

"As it always has happened before, with the two of you working on a plan together, something interesting always comes out of it. I know from personal experience how this works."

They both laughed, thinking the same thing and remembering the time Bev and Linda were in charge of a sorority party in college. They had needed security to prevent partygoers from leaving the building with cups of beer. This was always a problem at these parties, and they had a plan to prevent this problem. Their solution was to bring in David and some of his softball team friends to guard the windows and doors. By the end of the night there was one broken nose (not the softball guys), two Holiday Inn windows shot out (BB's) and a police escort for the entire security detail to the state line while one of the guys yelled out the window, "They may hate us in Valpo, but they love us in the Windy City". Sometimes things just get carried away.

David and Linda approached Pier 290, their favorite restaurant located on the lake and headed for "their" table overlooking the dock. The heat from the fireplace was just enough warmth to make it comfortable to eat outside. As regulars they knew the menu and all the wait staff. Instantly, Clark appeared at their table with two Diet Pepsis.

"Hi", Clark smiled. "Good to see you guys still out on a beautiful November evening."

"Better than sitting in front of the TV all night" Linda replied. "You know we can't resist the fish fry." That's what I'll have, but baked, with potato pancakes and apple sauce.

David ordered a bacon cheeseburger and a bowl of cream of broccoli soup. Wilson found his spot under the table and stretched out to relax. They all settled in for a last look at the lake before darkness fell. Linda loved these quiet nights when the restaurant fireplace glowed and there were only a few diners.

She reviewed her ideas for communications at LF and David asked. "What are you going to do about advertising beyond the newsletter? If you want almost everyone to be at the fundraiser, you will need some strong advertising messages and probably some way to plan messages that spread by word of mouth."

Linda tapped her finger on her fork and thought this over. "The LF club with the biggest membership is the golf and tennis club. I think we will have to post flyers at the clubhouse and in the locker rooms and we can have people mention it at the various leagues. Bev knows everyone in the leagues since she was the organizer of the drills for a couple of years. This will be a good way to casually bring up the fundraiser in conversation and get a read on the interest level."

"Yes, that is a good approach. If you can get some key people to attend, they will talk it up with their groups. It would also be a good idea to leak out a secret celebrity that is scheduled to make an appearance. Nothing like a secret to get everyone interested!"

"That's another great idea," Linda exclaimed, pulling out her phone to make a note of it. "I will work out a plan and schedule for a couple of information leaks at strategic times. We can then formally confirm them in the newsletter pieces later. This will get everyone buzzing."

Just then dinner arrived, and they shifted to talking about David's upcoming golf trip. On the way home Linda said, "I hope you realize that your support is so important to us as we go ahead with this plan. I love your ideas and we will probably need you help in ways I don't even know right now."

"I guess it's not possible to know it all right now since you are just getting started. You know you can count on me; I will be happy to do anything I can. This is no game, I think the possibility of this working is very good, so it is important to make the fullest effort to do it."

Wilson had gone ahead of them and was now sitting on the patio waiting for them to get home. They all headed in and turned on Netflix for a relaxing end to a beautiful day.

Chapter 12 – November 2019

It was a warm cloudy afternoon in central Florida and Bev was hard at work at her kitchen table. Her face was a study in concentration as she slowly but methodically added items to her Operation Lifesaver to-do list. The table was already littered with legal pads containing additional lists as well as brochures, pamphlets, and various scraps of paper and post-its with scribbled notes. She glanced at the clutter and smiled. Linda, she knew with absolute certainty, would have everything on her laptop, organized logically in virtual folders each titled with an equally logical moniker. But jumbled-up-disarray was more Bev's style and she knew that somehow it worked for her.

There were quite a few items checked off. The biggest by far was obtaining permissions and a rental agreement for holding the fundraiser at the on-site conference center. This had been a huge undertaking with many more hoops to jump through than Bev or Linda had anticipated. While the LF Board was enthusiastic about the idea of an event honoring in their words "The Greatest Leader in the Free World", there was so much red tape regarding insurance, liability, etc. For a while, Bev thought that Operation Lifesaver was going to be dead in the water. Finally, the Board agreed, probably swayed at the end by the publicity the event would garner as the largest fundraiser in all of Florida for their revered leader. In lieu of rent, they had agreed to accept 40% of all ticket proceeds, which would encourage them to fully support and help publicize the event.

Another checked item on the list was more problematic from a personal point of view. Upon her return to Florida Bev had quietly registered as an official Republican. While she knew this was absolutely necessary for credibility, it felt like such a betrayal to everything she had stood for throughout her entire life. To stand up to any scrutiny regarding her apparent change of heart, Bev had been studying all the current politics from a Republican point of view. She found that so many policies reflected a sickening lack of compassion towards people in need and fostered wealth and opportunity primarily to the already privileged members of society. The hypocrisy of Driscoll's alliance with the Evangelical communities was especially galling. Driscoll's actions both past and present had little in common with any Christian values.

Bev's checklist went on for many pages, but two un-checked items worried her considerably. The first concerned the lies and duplicity that was going to be required. Bev, while not especially close to her LF neighbors, had made many casual friends. Her participation in the tennis and golf clubs had given her a large social group. Not all of them knew of Bev's political leanings, but some did. It was going to be awkward to explain her newfound enthusiasm for President Driscoll and she worried how believable she could possibly be. And then there was Edna. Of course, Bev wanted to confide in Edna, tell her the entire plan, and get her advice. But could she trust that if Edna's mind became cloudy and confused, she wouldn't blurt out the real reasons behind the fundraiser? Lately Edna had been lucid, but Bev wasn't sure if this was only a temporary improvement.

The second item of worry involved Bev's brother Matt. Matt had lived the last 30 years as a semi-recluse. He had given up a very lucrative but high-pressure job in the IT industry to live a quiet solitary life in the north woods of Wisconsin. He had turned into a big burly fellow who wore flannel shirts and shorts half-way through the football season – just like any good Wisconsin Badger. Bev knew that he had kept up with all the technological advances within the industry, but she wasn't sure if he had the expertise to lead this particular project and if so, whether he could be convinced to join. Likely it would mean a temporary move to Florida.

Matt hated Florida. He felt that the entire state was a holding cell for wealthy geriatrics waiting to expire. He disliked the lack of a real winter, the preponderance of both Republicans and unrelenting sunshine, and he especially despised LF. Matt and Bev had always been close, both as kids and later as adults. Even though separated by many miles and lifestyle differences, they still talked several times a week. Matt had always been a reliable sounding board and though he rarely left his northern cabin, he somehow seemed to have a real grasp of Bev's life as well as that of her kids. Bev released a big sigh and reluctantly reached for her phone. She promised herself a large goblet of Cabernet if she completed this phone call and a large bowl of peppermint ice cream if he didn't immediately hang up on her.

Three very long hours later Bev gingerly unstuck the phone from her ear. She felt that she had just been through a protracted battle of arguments, counterarguments, pleas, bribes, and finally tears. But she had not only earned a bucket of Cabernet, a vat of ice cream, but so much more. Matt was coming to Florida! There was no guarantee that he would stay or even participate, but he would come and assess the state of the software and hardware at LF. He conceded that he would at least give his expert opinion

73

on if and how this operation could be pulled off, from a technical point of view. Bev knew that Linda could handle the organization, communication and scheduling. She herself could drum up the excitement needed to fill the convention hall, but all the technological components needed a real expert and Matt was coming to Florida!

Chapter 13 – December 2019

The campus was in a hurry for these last weeks of the semester. There were papers to grade, enrollment to track, adjunct faculty to hire for the spring term and Linda was in high gear, pushing to get it all done. If unexpected emergencies did not end up dumped on her desk, she would focus and get it all done, just as she always did. Commencement was next week and then it would settle down for the winter break.

This year Linda had purchased David's Christmas gift back in October, which was highly unusual. They would finally be seeing the hit play Hamilton down in the city – something they had put off due to the crazy price of tickets. Now the price was in range and Linda was sure David would be both surprised and pleased to go to the show.

This year had been extremely busy more than usual due to the work Bev and Linda were doing on Operation Lifesaver. Great progress was being made and with each step, their confidence that the plan would work was building. Bev's brother Matt was in place at LF and had gotten started with his IT work by developing an inventory of technology and devices across the LF property.

According to the spreadsheet, there were 65 security cameras on the property. These were mainly located in the obvious places such as the four security gates on to the property, the golf course entrance and patio, the pool exercise center, and two in the association offices. There had been a few unexpected cameras that Matt had found though. One was on the path to the lake, by the boat house. It would have been easy to miss that one since hardly anyone went down there since the new harbor was built. The other one was likely due to the association president wanting extra security on the garage where he kept his antique car. Several residents stored cars in a garage at the south end of the property and visitors were infrequent.

Linda smiled to herself and thought how smart it had been to get this inventory and it seemed perfectly reasonable for Matt to undertake this inventory as he was new to the job. There would probably be more things that he could do which would be very useful using his status of a recent hire as cover.

Beyond these cameras, more were placed to provide a look up and down each main street. Once someone pulled out of their driveway and reached the main street in their subdivision, it was possible to track them all the way to the village center and to the exits from the gated community. There was no sneaking around, on to or off the property.

Beyond the official security cameras, individual homes also had their own security, although Linda couldn't see why that would be necessary. Life on LF was all in its own bubble and anything or anyone not belonging to the community would stick out and be immediately noticed. Matt had informed them that 55% of individual units had additional security. These all had to be registered with the association. Most of these were doorbell cameras and cameras overlooking the back door and patio area. Since Operation Lifesaver would take place on the property, Linda did not see these as being an issue. However, anyone coming in to work at the event would be recorded entering and leaving the LF property. This meant that they would have to provide plausible deniability and keep the staff working the event in the dark about Operation Lifesaver. Matt had discovered that digital recordings from the cameras were downloaded to a cloud storage space where they were kept for two weeks. Recordings were purged daily so that there was always two weeks of footage saved.

Next on the list for the technology inventory was to track all devices keeping time. This included clocks, but is also included microwaves, refrigerators, and any other smart devices which used time. Matt was methodically tracking all of this – it would take him a few more months to make sure he had it all covered.

Last week a major step in Operation Lifesaver had fallen into place. Linda had contacted Mark, the cruise director from their recent trip to see if he could help them with the fundraiser. The last night of the cruise, Mark had led the travelers in a boisterous, entertaining game that drew everyone in to singing along, dancing and even some solo karaoke performances. He had a natural talent for identifying who was willing to participate and who the extroverts were so that the game could reach the outer limits of fun for everyone. This was exactly what they needed for the fundraiser and it was a critical element to make the plan work.

Mark was initially surprised to hear from Linda, but as she explained the fundraiser to him, he began to warm to the idea. His cruise schedule was over for the year and he returned to the US for the two months of November and December each year to be with his family. This would match up with the date for the fundraiser, but he was not sure he wanted to get involved in a fundraiser for Driscoll. Mark's job would be to act as Master of Ceremonies for the 24 hours of the fundraiser. Linda explained the basics of the event and the need to have participation in hourly events from as many people as possible to engage them completely – to the point where they lost track of time. They wanted nobody to go home early. He had agreed to hear more of the details, so they scheduled time for a video call with Bev. Linda was confident that Bev could use her persuasive powers from her days as a journalist to convince Mark to support their plan.

Later that week, Linda was back at the lake and preparing for their follow-up call. She had her talking points prepared and this time she and Bev would have to let Mark in on the real event going on behind the scenes. On the cruise, Mark had been supremely professional, but Linda picked up several comments about Brexit and US politics that made her wonder about his true feelings on politics. She felt sure that, underneath his professionalism he had a mischievous side and maybe even activist leanings. If she had him pegged correctly, he might be a good partner they could depend on to support the true mission of the fundraiser.

At noon Linda logged on and soon she and Bev were waiting for Mark to call in. He joined shortly and they started out with a pleasant conversation so everyone could get reacquainted. Mark was a big, blond, vivacious man with a huge store of energy and enthusiasm. Along with his typical British accent his charismatic personality was supported by his practice of focusing intently on the person speaking. This was probably a necessary talent as a cruise director to make sure guests felt their concerns were being heard and so that he could intuit their needs both spoken and unspoken.

"Well it is a pleasure to speak with you ladies today. I remember your group on our cruise in August. Such a marvelous time we all had, didn't we?" Mark smiled into the screen. "As I recall some were of the more sedate variety – not that everyone did not enjoy themselves – and others, (who shall remain nameless) had a penchant for imbibing and dancing. In fact, they might have been convinced without too much effort to do just about anything! Who would ever have guessed that ballroom dancing skills would be called upon, but there you have it. Anyway, it worked out to make for a week well-spent, didn't it?"

"We had the time of our lives on the trip. The crew saw to our every need and you had everything organized and perfectly planned. I know there was a lot of work going on behind the scenes. For instance, it is mind-blowing to think of how many dishes must be washed every day." Bev said. "I thought it was amazing that everyone took their excursions, nobody got lost, all meals were perfectly prepared and served. A lot of work goes into it and that level of excellence doesn't just happen by accident."

"Well of course that is our specialty. We keep everything sorted so you don't have to. I understand you have a new adventure planned where I can be of service, don't you? Shall we discuss the particulars?"

"Yes", Linda began, "Let's get down to details. When we spoke last week, I described our fundraiser event. It will be the biggest event of the year for LF. We expect more than 80,000 people to attend. The venue is the convention center on the property. This is often used to offer the residents concerts and shows, lectures from famous people, and political rallies." Linda paused for a second to let the size of the task sink in.

Mark's eyebrows raised and he leaned back in his chair to digest these details. Bev picked it up, "It will be a political fundraiser supporting the second inauguration of our President. People in LF voted overwhelmingly for him the first time and when he comes to town, they fill the convention center to hear his speeches.

Mark's face remained completely neutral as he listened further. Linda continued, "Here's the interesting part, it's not really a fundraiser in support of the President, it is really what we are calling Operation Lifesaver. Our goal with this event is to pass it off as a fundraiser, while all the time it is really an event designed to engage as many people as possible, create an event where time is misrepresented so that everyone thinks it is a 12-hour event, when really it is a 24-hour event.

Mark cocked his head sideways trying to understand. He slowly absorbed the impact of the time difference.

"Yes, Bev continued, "This is not so much a fundraiser as it is a plot to confuse time so that the attendees miss their opportunity to vote in the election. They will think the party went on all night ending at 7:00 am. Instead, each hour will become 2 hours and the event will really end at 7:00 pm after the polls close."

Mark leaned in giving them a close-up of his face and squinted at the screen. "Do I understand that you ladies are endeavoring to pull off a caper that will influence the outcome of the election?"

"Precisely, "Linda exclaimed, "how clever of you to see the point. These are desperate times, and everyone must do what they can as a patriot. Those boobs in DC can't get anything done and we are likely to have to put up with this idiot for another four years if someone doesn't do something. This is only a small contribution, but according to our research, it could be enough to impact the vote for Florida and we all know the past regarding Florida and presidential elections."

"This could be big" said Bev, "but it needs to not look big and it must not reveal its real purpose."

Bev went on using all her skills and experience as a journalist to persuade Mark to participate. Linda had always been amazed how Bev could entice nearly anyone to agree to an interview or share their life secrets in a matter of minutes. While Linda was more reserved, Bev made friends effortlessly. People, whether they be potential interviewees, acquaintances or close friends could sense that Bev was genuinely interested in their life stories and they responded with, what Linda felt were, startlingly personal admissions. This empathy had served her well as a journalist and also made her an extraordinary friend.

Mark's mouth hung open slightly as he worked to grasp this information and fully understand all the implications. He immediately began to think of the practical details for pulling it off. "Well, on the surface, I have to congratulate you ladies on a brilliant and diabolical plan. It's subtle, yet right to the point, isn't it? Of course, we will need to work out a million details, won't we?" Like cost, agenda, and even our getaway at the end!" Mark was beginning to think of himself as part of the team already.

"It sounds like you are on board with the idea Mark. We were hoping this would not scare you off and we wanted to get your thoughts on the feasibility. Where could we go wrong, we need to think about all the possible ways this thing could derail. You are an expert in planning the logistics of events, so your acceptance of our proposal is important. Of course, we have many details to work out including your fee. We have about one year to pull this off. Do you think we can do it?"

"I'm pleased to accept the challenge and ideas are already bubbling up in my head. Count me in!"

Chapter 14 – December 2019

Bev woke up early that December 10th morning. After a bracing cup of hot English Breakfast tea, she began to rummage in the storage closet located in the garage. It took a while but eventually she located the two large boxes marked Christmas decorations. She winced to see Harry's handwriting on the boxes and remembered all the happy Christmases of years' past. Harry had pretended to be a curmudgeon with the kids about the holidays, but he had always been the first to suggest a snowball fight or a drive to find the gaudiest yard decorations in the neighborhood. He was the one to insist on Christmas stockings even when the kids were long past childhood. And he was the one that always picked out the most perfect Christmas present for Bev. She smiled when she thought of the year he tried to sneak in a kayak for Bev and paddleboards for the kids, banging around so much that every dog in the neighborhood started barking. The absolute best gift had been the year he presented her with a stack of books, each the first in a series featuring a woman detective. This would be the first Christmas since she lost her dearest friend and life companion that she would decorate for the holidays. But in the spirit of healing and moving ahead with her life, she was determined to jump on the Christmas bandwagon.

Bev heard a sharp rap on her kitchen door and opened it to find an unlikely trio: Matt, Edna, and Miguel. When Matt had visited in November, he had discovered that sunshine and warm days might not be such a bad thing. And when he had met Edna, they inexplicably hit it off. Both were somewhat taciturn and antisocial and by choice had lived most of their lives alone. They seemed to share the same cynical point of view and sarcastic sense of humor. Since meeting Matt, Edna's mental cloudiness had abated and when it did appear, Matt was uncharacteristically patient and tolerant. Matt had decided that Edna could indeed be trusted, at least with the big picture, and she was now acting as his unofficial assistant. It turned out, somewhat to Bev's embarrassment, that Edna was pretty savvy with computers, much more so than Bev.

Miguel was the latest addition to the Operation Lifesaver IT team. Miguel was the 11-year-old son of Marisol and Jose Martinez, a couple who had emigrated from Todas Santos Mexico and were live-in employees at LF. Jose was the night guard at the main entrance and Marisol worked in the conference center kitchens. Miguel, small with dark hair and eyes and a big mischievous smile, was a computer savant. His goal in life was to "grow up to be a computer hacker". In fact, Miguel was currently on a 3-day suspension from 6th grade after "tinkering" (his words) with school software so that the hourly bell was replaced by the heavy metal sounds of Metallica. The principal was neither amused nor impressed by Miguel's ability nor was he a Metallica fan, so Miguel was at loose ends when Matt discovered him "tinkering" with the security system by the conference center. Matt immediately recognized a kindred spirit as well as a valuable asset. The trio of Matt, a burly bespectacled transplant from the cold north woods, Edna who had the reputation as a befuddled ex-hippy and an impish, brilliant Hispanic lad was an unlikely force of technological destruction and would likely pass unnoticed and underestimated.

Miguel spoke up in his high childish voice "Hiya Miss Bev. We finished overriding the television satellite software. Got any more of those Oreos?"

"Sure, come on in, all of you. Edna, why are you wearing that wig?"

"Just trying out some disguises for the big day."

Matt broke in impatiently "Big sis, I wish you had told us that the LF satellite system for the television was interfaced with the cell service. We could have been done hours ago."

Bev shrugged "Matt, how the heck would I have known that? I'm lucky if I can click enough buttons on my television remote so I can watch reruns of Cagney and Lacey. So, whatever you managed to do, how does it impact Operation Lifesaver?"

Matt sighed, visibly attempting to be patient with his technologically backward sister. "It's all about controlling the television programming for the Monday night before the election. Not everyone will attend the fundraiser you know Bev. Although I totally believe in your persuasive abilities to fill up the conference center. After all, here I am due to those talents." He chuckled before continuing, "So for those folks at home we need to keep them distracted. They need to be tuned into television shows that will keep their attention. And what's more riveting than a movie marathon? We will have three channels running these marathons. One marathon dedicated to Alfred Hitchcock movies, one to old classics like *Casablanca* and *Gone With the Wind*, and my personal favorite marathon: The Three Stooges."

Bev smiled and then asked, "But what about people that are news junkies? The ones that are glued to Fox news?"

"I have a special treat for them, a marathon of the greatest moments in Republican history since the days of Eisenhower. I'm making a montage of speeches, biographies, debate clips etc. Enough to keep their beady little Republican eyes glued to the set for 24 hours."

Miguel added, "Uncle Matt is letting me do the splicing. It's pretty easy, but if I don't make any mistakes, he said I could help with the clocks. Uncle Matt is figuring how we can keep all the clocks in LF synchronized to Operation Lifesaver time. And gosh there are a bazillion clocks...not just regular clocks but on microwaves, on tablets, and cell phones – just everywhere."

Edna added while looking fondly at Matt "Your brother is so smart it's scary."

Matt reddened and replied gruffly "Most fun I've had in 20 years. Lots of this is pretty basic; the Conference Center's clocks are all digital but controlling the time on everyone's personal devices will be trickier."

Reminded of the time, Bev glanced at the microwave clock and exclaimed "Hey, I have to fly – the Victory for Driscoll committee meeting starts in 20 minutes."

The Victory for Driscoll committee (abbreviated to VFD) met every 2 weeks. At first Bev was afraid that this committee would completely derail the Operation Lifesaver, but it turned out to be just the opposite. Both the community board and the conference center had insisted that Bev be "assisted" by long time community members (staunch Republicans, of course). When they slowly took over the planning of the event, Bev was certain the end was near. However, the committee gave Bev the anonymity she needed to stay in the shadows. Plus, the committee was doing all the grunt work that Bev would have been totally unequipped to handle on her own. Many of the members had put on fundraisers in the past, although none as huge as this one was planned to be. Bev was able to volunteer for several jobs that would be key to the success of Operation Lifesaver, most importantly, the responsibility of procuring a Master of Ceremonies for the event. And the machinations of Matt, Edna, Miguel as well as Linda up north could continue in parallel with the committee's work. It was ironic that the efforts of the VFT committee would be paramount to the success of Operation Lifesaver. If Operation Lifesaver were a success and Driscoll lost the Florida electoral vote, his defeat could be attributed to the hard work of the dedicated Republicans at LF.

Chapter 15- January 2020

"If that perfect phone call with the President of Ukraine Isn't considered appropriate, then no future President can EVER again speak to another foreign leader!"

"...Trump's squandered economic opportunities are, of course, secondary at this point to his de facto self-impeachment. Trump has managed to make things clear enough for everyone to understand. First he demanded that foreign regimes produce dirt on domestic political rivals, not just in phone calls but right there on camera. Now he's engaged in a crude, obvious effort to stonewall the House impeachment inquiry that is clearly an impeachable offense in itself.

27 Sep 2019, Paul Krugman, New York Times

The commuter train to Chicago approached slowly, maybe a minute early due to the coming holiday and many people taking the day off. You wouldn't think it would make a difference, but the effect was for the train to be a minute early "due to passenger loading". This was just enough to catch a few people who found themselves having to make a run for it and cross the tracks as the train approached. It was amazing the risk people were willing to take when the next train would arrive in only twenty minutes.

Linda turned to look the other direction and saw the early sunrise. The sky was just beginning to turn pink at the very bottom. She purposely did not watch the running passengers in preparation for the day when one would inevitably miscalculate. She refused to be a witness to the terrible result. Well, it would not be today, Linda reflected as the train pulled to a stop and the doors opened right in front of where she stood.

Linda noticed a man rudely cut in front of the woman who had been patiently waiting next to her. She recognized him: he was a regular commuter who knew the routine and yet felt fine about not waiting his turn. By cutting the woman off, he was first to board on that side and quickly climbed upstairs where there was a rich supply of seats available. Linda often wondered why someone would behave this way. Didn't they have any ability to see how obnoxious they were or just the common courtesy to take their turn? He was the same type that would settle into a complete "man spread" encroaching on the space of people next to him. The world was full of them.

That evening she and David packed one suitcase for their four-day trip to visit Bev. This would be only the second time Linda had seen LF for herself. David was mainly interested in the rounds of golf they had booked, and they were both looking forward to some warm days to break up the midwest winter.

Linda enjoyed traveling, although she did not miss her consulting days where travel was a weekly routine. Their flight was on time and as they exited the terminal in Orlando, Bev was waiting and waved them over to her car. They all hugged and quickly jumped in and Bev circled out, taking them back to LF.

After a relaxing lunch on the patio, Bev took them on a tour of the property.

"Here are the tennis courts. You can see they are converting some to pickleball. It's very popular, but you know me, I love to hear the pop of hitting a tennis ball."

"I see the golf course," David said as they turned the corner. "It looks to be in good shape. We will get our season off to an early start this year."

"Up ahead on the right you will see the convention center." Bev pointed across the windshield. They drove into the parking lot and slowly cruised around the enormous structure.

"This is massive," Linda exclaimed thoughtfully, "I can easily see how it will accommodate the number we are expecting for the fundraiser."

It was actually very similar to the Orlando convention center used for the healthcare conference Linda had attended several times. Maybe not quite as big, but apparently it would at least fit the 80,000 people they were expecting. She took a few pictures in case there was a question later and so she could forward them on to Mark.

After taking a brief tour inside, Linda saw how the infrastructure that was in place and used for other events would work for their plan. Food service was accounted for, bathrooms, multiple large conference rooms that could hold at least 1000 people, and the great ball room which would be the spot for guest celebrities to make their appearances and performances. Linda had already completed signed contracts with two of the three celebrities they had contacted. These special performances would be critical for capturing the interest of LF residents and would be used to help with the deception on time that was so integral to their plan.

Satisfied, Linda asked, "Were there any questions that came up when the committee approved signing the contract for the Center this week?"

"As usual, we did hear from Eric who raised some good questions for the committee to discuss. He wanted to know who was paying the deposit. I explained that our charitable fund will take care of that – and we will be reimbursed by the proceeds from tickets bought. Then Edna raised a general question about how we would sell the tickets. This gave us another chance to talk about the purpose of the fundraiser in more depth so I was able to reiterate that it would support the second inauguration of the president." Bev smiled slyly at this. "As it turns out, Eric attended the first inauguration - the one with the "biggest attendance ever" –and so he reminisced about how wonderful it was and actually stoked the excitement of the whole committee."

"Sometimes you get extra help you could not have planned for," Linda said. "It's nice to have these lucky breaks along the way to get an extra boost."

They glided back up Bev's driveway and headed in the house. Gazing up and down the street, Linda was struck by the homogeneous look of each house. They were all beautiful, but they were almost identical. She took note of Bev's house number and reminded herself to bring her phone if she and David went for a walk, in case they got lost. They decided to relax for a few hours by the pool before going to the golf club for dinner.

Refreshed from their quiet afternoon, Bev, David and Linda headed out for an early dinner. It turned out not to be too early for much of the crowd was already there when they arrived. Luckily, Bev had reserved a table because, at 5:30, the restaurant was nearly full. The hostess seated them next to the window overlooking the 18th green.

"This is a perfect view, "David enthused. "We can see the final golfers of the day finishing up."

"I specifically asked for this table" Bev said. "It also gives us a strategic view of the whole room so I can point out various key people for you to see. There's Edna over at the table by the fountain. She is the one in the purple kaftan. David, will you order the drinks so I can go introduce Linda?"

"Of course," David agreed. "Sauvignon Blanc for Linda and Bacardi and Diet Pepsi for you right Bev?"

"You've got it!" Bev replied as she pushed back her chair and led the way over to Edna, who was alone at her table. "Hi Edna, I want you to meet my longtime friend Linda from Chicago. She's visiting me for a few days and I'm showing her around the property. She is also helping me with the fundraiser."

"Pleased to meet you, Linda. Smart of you to be escaping the cold winter for a few days. The weather is one of our best features down here at LF."

"When did you move here?" Linda asked.

"I've lived here for many years," Edna said as she squinted to remember. "As you're exploring, make sure you see our fine theater where we as a community put on three plays each year. I have been lucky enough to land a minor role in many of them and always at least participate in the chorus if it is a musical."

"Edna is a musician with a background in piano and voice performance," Bev filled in. "We are lucky to have someone with her talent and dedication to theater."

"That sounds wonderful. I will be sure to investigate the theater, thanks for mentioning it. I think I see drinks arriving at our table. So nice to meet you Edna."

Edna waved as they returned to their table and an older gentleman came up to speak with her.

"She seems like a nice person of get to know." Linda remarked.

"I really think she is an interesting person with many different talents. There are rumors though that her mind drifts and that she may be developing dementia. She always can be counted on to pitch in such as she is doing on the fundraiser committee. She was first to accept my invitation."

"Welcome back ladies, your drinks have arrived." David motioned for them to be seated. "I think I'll have a bacon cheeseburger.

After dinner they took a short walk over to the gigantic pool and exercise center. Linda found all the machines that she liked to use in her workouts. The pool looked inviting. Even though it was after dinner, the temperature was still in the 70's, much warmer than January in Chicago. Small groups of women and some couples were out sitting by the pool with after dinner drinks. The lights came on and set a beautiful ambiance for a quiet evening relaxing outside. Gazing around, Linda was struck by the vast difference between this environment and the one she spent her working days in at the university.

Her daily experience blended people of diverse races, cultural backgrounds and ages. As she looked around the pool, she thought back on what she had seen today on the LF property. Nothing but gray hair and mainly white skin. It was a very homogenous group with little variety. One good thing about that was that it disguised the effect of the "invisible old person." Linda had become more sensitive to this phenomenon after reading an article about how many older people, especially women "of a certain age", report that people treat them like they are invisible. They don't notice old people or maybe it was that they don't find the need to recognize an older person.

Here, in this environment, where everyone was old, that whole effect was gone. But the lack of diversity created an artificial environment to some extent. Yes, the LF residents had chosen to be here, and it was not unpleasant. But Linda appreciated the diversity in her world, especially if she could come home to David, the lake, and Wilson. She would have to mention this to Bev and get another perspective. She couldn't help feeling that they needed to think about how these issues might influence the outcome of their plans.

Chapter 16 – February 2020

"We're losing our damn minds": I'll just say it this way: The fate of the world depends on the Democrats getting their shit together and winning in November. We have to beat Trump. And so far, I don't like what I see." James Carville

Sean Illing, Vox.com Feb 7, 2020

Bev woke to the sounds of a driving rain hitting the windows and roof. Thunder rolled in the distance. Hopefully the storm was moving eastward, although it felt cozy to lay in her bed watching the palm trees sway in the winds. She allowed herself a bit of a lazy morning. January had been full of activity – first Linda and David down ostensibly for a golf weekend but really to become acquainted with the layout of the conference center. Bev was glad that Linda had met Edna. They seemed to recognize in each other a shared no-nonsense way of approaching life. Linda had also met with Matt and gone over many of the IT issues. Bev and David had sat together both feeling left out of the conversation as Matt and Linda had conferred on, using words, abbreviations, and acronyms that were totally foreign. Linda had raised her eyebrows when she learned of Miguel's involvement but after just a few minutes with him, Linda was both charmed and impressed.

The IT team was making good progress. They had tackled the television programming for both the Monday and Tuesday of Election Day and had an idea for rerouting the Fox radio news feed that blared incessantly in the town squares throughout the day. While controlling the digital clocks within the conference center was easily accomplished, the problem of controlling all the clocks located within the homes was trickier. Matt planned to force a short power outage throughout the community which would disrupt the time sequence. When the clocks were reset, they would automatically adhere to the Operation Lifesaver time. As for cell phones, Matt would use an electromagnetic pulse to create a dead zone within the conference center. But he and the team were uncertain as to how to manipulate the time on the cell phones, tablets, and laptops used within LF.

Bev glanced at the clock and realized that she needed to get dressed soon if she were to make the 11:00 committee meeting. Bev smiled to herself when she thought of the committee, self-named Victory for Driscoll. At present, the VFT group consisted of 12 members – 10 staunch Republicans plus Bev and Edna. Bev and Edna likened themselves to covert spies, infiltrating the fervent conservatives as moles. Bev sometimes worried that Edna might have one of her confused spells and go walkabout, but Edna had been consistently lucid. In fact, she had the knack for asking questions that prompted the group into making just exactly the decision that would most benefit Operation Lifesaver. Last week when the committee had questioned Bev on her hiring of Viking Cruise Director Mark Williams as the Master of Ceremonies, Edna had wondered aloud if Mark's British accent wouldn't make the whole event a bit posher? Soon, everyone was congratulating each other as to how upscale this whole event was shaping up to be.

Of the other ten members, eight were white men, two white women; a ratio which seemed to reflect the metrics of the entire Driscoll administration. Bev reminded herself that just because these ten, as well as the majority of the LF residents were Republican, this didn't make them bad people or even unlikeable. At times, she felt tremendous guilt that she, Edna, Linda, and Matt were working to undermine their efforts. There were even times when Bev felt a fellowship with many on the committee. One woman, Patricia, had invited Bev to her home on several occasions. Patricia was also a widow. She and her husband, both attorneys, had lived in Washington DC, enjoying life in high society filled with galas and fundraisers, mostly to benefit the Bush administration. It was her expertise with high-level fundraising that was ensuring the success of the LF November event.

As Bev grew to know Patricia, she found they had much in common. They had both relocated to LF at the urging of their golf-obsessed husbands, and then found themselves alone and far away from the lives they had loved further north. Patricia had confided in Bev that while she despised Driscoll the man, she supported his economic and trade policies. Although she was appalled that families had been separated at the border, she firmly believed that the country's lax immigration policies from years' past had resulted in a system that was out of control and strong measures were needed.

Patricia felt that illegal immigrants should not be issued drivers licenses or receive free health care, food stamps or public education. She sympathized with the immigrant's quest for a better life for their children but adamantly felt that only legal U.S. citizens should receive these benefits.

Patricia was firm in her political beliefs but never derisive towards other views. She simply felt that a Democratic congress encouraged too much federal oversight in the lives of American citizens. The current strong economy and low unemployment were also factors, although Patricia conceded that this might not be all a result of the current administration.

Politics aside, Bev enjoyed Patricia's company. She was funny, intelligent and shared Bev's predilection for a crisp gin and tonic at the end of a long day. After spending a lively evening together, talking about books, plays, and travel, Bev would lie awake for hours, knowing that Patricia would likely despise her once the ramifications of Operation Lifesaver were revealed on Wednesday, November 4.

For that matter, what was the exit plan for Bev, Edna and Matt? Everyone working on Operation Lifesaver was so caught up in pulling this off that little had been said about what would come after. Even if the operation failed and Driscoll did get Florida's electoral votes, every Republican at LF would know that they had been the target of a plan to cheat them of their votes. It had all sounded so straightforward and justifiable on that autumn night last summer. Now Bev was feeling uncertain about the morality of the whole plan and she knew it was way too late to put the brakes on. Over 10,000 tickets had been sold for the big event, and contracts had already been signed for several celebrities. Yes, no matter what qualms she had, Operation Lifesaver and Victory for Driscoll were on a collision course.

Chapter 17 – March 2020

Wisconsin spice company spends more than $100,000 on pro- impeachment ads

"I think people are starting to wake up and starting to actually see who this president is,"

Penzeys Spices, a Wauwatosa-based spice company, spent $109,933 posting and reposting an ad that called Trump's phone call with Ukranian President Volodymyr Zelensky a "mandatory open and shut case for the impeachment."

The post has gotten nearly 250,000 likes and 43,000 shares, tipping it into "viral" territory in the realm of social media. "This one seems to have really caught a wind," Penzey said.

Laurel White, wpr.org, 16 Dec. 2019

Life at the lake was still in quiet winter mode and Linda was getting restless. After five months of dark and cold, the mornings were once again bright and sunny, but just one step outside and the wind and 30-degree temperatures were a quick reminder that winter was not over yet. On her Wednesday call with Bev, they had sidetracked into a discussion about the impact of the impeachment vote. Avoiding removal from office meant that the election was now more crucial than ever. Although the House had upheld its constitutional responsibility by completing articles of impeachment, Driscoll could now use his acquittal in the Senate as support for asking for interference from foreign governments in the US election process. He had legitimized a new low for the future and there was no telling the lasting damage it might cause.

During the past week Linda had made tremendous progress on the fundraiser. She and Bev developed a detailed time chart for the whole 12/24-hour period. There would be a kickoff event at Eastern Standard (EST) time 7:00 pm. A "red carpet" would be set up for participants to enter and show off their finery. Advanced ticket sales at a reduced price was working out well and they already had over 30,000 tickets sold. It seems that early communications had the desired effect to stir up interest. That also provided them with funding to sign contracts with the event celebrities.

The first celebrity performance would be two hours later at official time 9:00 pm EST or 8:00 pm Operation Lifesaver (OL) Time. This would be Rachel Stone, the country western singer. She was a high energy performer that would get everyone dancing. A gigantic dance floor would be installed in the grand ballroom where a dance competition would take place. Mid-sized conference rooms all had giant screens which would be used to make the performance visible to all attendees, no matter where they were in the conference center. Mark would emcee the dance competition.

They had settled on installing a program into the internal server clock that would move the clock at half the normal speed. Time = Time X 1/2. This plan would lead to a steady time change inside the conference center that would allow them to show clicks and time to all attendees. Every EST minute would equal two OL minutes. This gradual slowing down of time would probably not be noticeable for the first 3-4 hours, but after that, there could be some people who would begin to feel the time drag. Linda's own internal clock was rarely off by more than 15 minutes, so it was probably true that others had a natural feel for time. Communication about the fundraiser talked about how the whole event would take place over 12 hours with performance, raffles, competitions, and games occurring every hour. The design of the program was carefully timed and planned to build to a crescendo at the end.

For this reason, they had explored the option of pumping oxygen into the conference center. The physiological effect would be to freshen everyone up and keep everyone from feeling tired. Although they had heard this was a trick used by casinos, some research into this showed that it was a myth that casinos pumped oxygen in so that players would stay awake and play longer. It would cost millions to pump oxygen through the HVAC system, not to mention the fire hazard of pure oxygen. Casinos did however use "oxygen bars" and sold portable recreational oxygen canisters that players could purchase. Linda and Bev decided that the fundraiser would do like the casinos and provide oxygen bars and each couple would get portable oxygen canister the size of a 12 oz water bottle as part of their gift bag when they arrived. This way, the use of oxygen was not a secret, a concern in terms of deception and possible backlash once people found out what had happened. Everyone would be fully aware of taking the oxygen so there were no legal or ethical concerns.

The O^2 bars were a stroke of genius that enabled them to promote use of oxygen openly and encourage use. "For people who play and party hard" and in this case, for people trying to stay awake for 24 hours. They would have a team of oxygen bar volunteers that would rotate through the six stations. The coordinator of this group was Susan, a pickleball regular and retired nurse. She had come to Bev back in January and volunteered her services for supporting the fundraiser. Susan was just what they needed to oversee the oxygen. With her clinical background, she could answer questions people might have. Her personality was no-nonsense, fun, energetic – she was a karaoke regular and swam for 30 minutes every day. She was fearless after having served in Vietnam for two years and was always ready to do anything. Each year on her birthday she sky-dived to celebrate.

Susan did not know the whole plot behind the fundraiser, but she was smart and very aware of things going on around her. Bev and Linda discussed how she might very well begin to notice what was going on, so they knew a strategy was needed to either bring her in ahead of time or to break it to her during the fundraiser at some point. Linda was in favor of waiting as long as possible, before telling Susan everything. At the same time, it was important to having her support to tell Susan before she found out on her own. They decided to say that her role was important to the mission of the fundraiser – it was not just fun and games – and that they would be counting on her. Then they would reveal more details to emphasize _how_ important it was during the evening and at midnight (12 hours in), they could reveal all. It was taking a risk, but they were betting Susan would be all in. She and her husband Bruce were Democrats after all.

Operation Lifesaver Timeline

EST	OLT	EST	OLT
7:00 **pm**	7:00 pm	7:00 **am**	1:00 am
8:00 pm	7:30 pm	8:00 am	1:30 am
9:00 pm	8:00 pm	9:00 am	2:00 am
10:00 pm	8:30 pm	10:00 am	2:30 am
11:00 pm	9:00 pm	11:00 am	3:00 am
12:00 midnight	9:30 pm	12:00 noon	3:30 am
1:00 am	10:00 pm	1:00 pm	4:00 am
2:00 am	10:30 pm	2:00 pm	4:30 am
3:00 am	11:00 pm	3:00 pm	5:00 am
4:00 am	11:30 pm	4:00 pm	5:30 am
5:00 am	midnight	5:00 pm	6:00 am
6:00 am	12:30	6:00 pm	6:30 am

Linda closed her notebook, done reviewing the plans for today. David would be home soon, and they were making pizzas for dinner. She stood in front of the master plan on the wall of her studio in the guest house. Bev was no longer visiting, but her work to spell out the plan along with her yellow sticky notes was still there and as they moved closer to their deadline, they were filling in the gaps to the plan.

Looking at the timeline, Linda could see that they were on track, but there was still more work to do on one key aspect of the event – the art auction. This would entail a visit to Naples with two goals: one, get out of the cold and enjoy some good weather and two, visit David's cousin Paul who ran a successful art gallery in downtown Naples. Paul and his wife Gwen had already agreed to be a part of the plan, but there were many details to work out. Linda smiled to herself and gazed out at the lake as she shut off the lights. Yes, she was definitely ready for a break and some warm weather. Bev would drive down and meet them in Naples next week.

Chapter 18 - March 2020

An Unsettling New Theory, There is No Swing Voter

"The Chuck Todd theory of American politics. "

"The idea that there is this informed, engaged American population that is watching these political events and watching their elected leaders and assessing their behavior and making a judgment."

David Freedlander, Politico Magazine, 02/06/2020

Bev hurriedly unlocked her door and rushed over to the portal, a few minutes late for her weekly virtual lunch date with Linda. When they made the video connection, Linda noticed Bev seemed out of breath.

"Yes, I'm a mess today," Bev answered, her face glistening with perspiration. "I ran from Eric's house - he's been haranguing me to turn in my receipts and to get him Mark's contract for master of ceremonies. He's probably the most irritating committee member, always harping on every minor financial point, always explaining and re-explaining like I'm an idiot who can't grasp the finer points of his glorious spreadsheet."

"I think the kids call that mansplaining" Linda chuckled "But he is an accountant and he's probably just dotting his I's and crossing his T's. What did he say about Mark?"

"Well he was ready to get all huffy about Mark's fee until I told him that Mark was such an ardent Driscoll supporter that he would give the committee a thirty percent discount for his services. That shut Eric up immediately."

"Well done Bev. I'll make sure to tell Mark that he really has to play up his supposed love of all things Driscoll."

Linda paused and studied Bev's face from her video screen 1200 miles away. Even at that distance, she could tell that Bev was upset about more than Eric's pompous attitude.

"Bev, what's wrong? Just be honest with me."

Bev's face crumbled and she started sobbing. "Linda, this is so much harder than I thought it would be."

"But Bev, everything is right on target. We have our timeline now and Matt, Edna, and Miguel have conquered most of our IT issues. Susan is helping with our oxygen bar and the entertainment is nearly all lined up. And ticket sales are fantastic. Next week we'll be in Naples and talking with David's cousin Paul about the art auction. It's all going great."

"Linda you don't understand what it's like for me down here. I'm beginning to realize how hated I'm going to be when this is over. I like a lot of these people. Except for Eric, the committee is fun, and everyone thinks we are all pulling together. But I know that isn't true at all. And I've lost all my old friends- even my golf partner in the league won't talk to me. They don't understand why I'm suddenly a Republican. Some of them are really getting fired up over the fundraiser. I'm worried that they will try to sabotage things, maybe even get violent. My neighbor Amy, who I used to play tennis with, is threatening to bring in the entire Florida Democratic League of Voters to block all the entrances of the conference center. And back when I was a Democrat, I would have applauded it. Now I must pretend that I completely disagree with her. I thought this would be all fun and exciting, like a spy from a Tom Clancy novel, and it was at first. But now I feel like a rat, and a lonely one at that."

"Bev you need a break and meeting David and me in Naples is just the remedy. I totally get that you are on the front lines of this battle. I understand that you are feeling conflicted. I firmly believe that Operation Lifesaver is a necessary and patriotic duty, but it's tough when that means betraying friends. Yes, a lot of people in LF will be very, very angry, but we are serving a greater good. This man is a tyrant and his presidency is doing great damage to our country. If we can aid in his removal, then we must accept some uncomfortable consequences I'll help you through this, I promise."

"Ok." Bev took in a great breath and wiped away her tears. "I'll handle it. And a week away from here is probably a good idea."

Bev and Linda chatted for a few more minutes, making plans for golfing and dinners out in Naples. When Bev disconnected her video feed, she was feeling a little bit better. Still a Benedict Arnold, but she knew that Linda would give her the emotional support that she needed to get through this.

Five days later, car packed with golf clubs, suitcases and coolers, Bev drove across the state to the upscale city of Naples. Bev was staying in a small bed and breakfast located in the older and very affluent center of Naples, a mere two blocks from the beach. Standing on the beautiful beach with the vast Gulf of Mexico shimmering in the sunlight, she realized how land locked LF was. It amazed her how popular LF was becoming, with the constant and unending construction of new homes, expanding the boundaries to welcome more and more snowbirds from the north. But the flat sparse interior of Florida was so unattractive compared to the gulf area. Less golf courses Bev conceded, but so much more natural beauty.

That afternoon Bev met Linda and David for an early dinner. Linda gave her a long and heartfelt embrace. The three enjoyed a seafood dinner on the patio of a gulf front restaurant chatting about family and mutual friends.

Bev felt herself relaxing; the knots in her back and stomach, near constant companions of late, loosened and she began to eat with relish. The grouper was fresh and expertly prepared and the crisp citrusy Sauvignon Blanc that David had chosen was the perfect accompaniment. When Bev found herself ordering key lime pie for dessert, she knew she was on the mend from the anxiety and uncertainty of the past few weeks. She allowed a wry smile when she realized that she hadn't indulged in sweets for months, a sure reaction to the turmoil. Her covert life in LF was good for the waistline even if her nerves had suffered.

Before saying goodnight, the three made plans for golf the next day at Raptor Bay, a gorgeous course in Bonita Springs that showcased the natural beauty of the surrounding estuary. They would enjoy another dinner and then meet with Paul, David's cousin, to finalize the plans for the art auction.

Walking back to her bed and breakfast, Bev thought about her dinner with Linda and David. She knew that Linda had deliberately steered the conversation away from any talk of Operation Lifesaver, and while Bev appreciated the respite, she knew she had come to a fork in the road. She either had to fully commit with eyes wide open to the endeavor, with all its possible consequences, or get out right now. The conflict between following through on the pact made with Linda last August on the river cruise and the personal ramifications that were inherent to this plan had to be resolved tonight.

It was true, Bev's friendship with Linda spanned many decades- her entire adult life in fact. They had been roommates in college and had remained the closest of friends, sisters really. Bev had always jumped in with total commitment and absolutely no reservations to all of Linda's schemes throughout college. So many nights in their tiny dorm room Linda would get a grand idea and Bev would reach for a notepad to capture all the details spilling excitedly and passionately out of Linda. Bev had always prided herself on her loyalty to Linda and her perfect record of saying "Yes!" even while worrying inside how she was going to finish all her schoolwork with this new distraction.

Their biggest and most ambitious project had been to start a new sorority on campus, one that would eschew the exclusivity and snobbism that defined the others. Bev remembered the countless hours spent on recruitment and planning and the subsequent all-nighters she had endured to keep up with her school assignments. There was more than one occasion when Bev had found herself running across campus at 5 AM to slip a paper under a professor's door before a deadline. Linda had always been a master of time management, her work done a week early without the frenzied time crunch that characterized Bev's work. The sorority was a great success and Bev had kept her grade point average up, but not without a herculean effort.

This project now, Operation Lifesaver, was not a college scheme. It was a serious attempt to impact election results and would likely have serious consequences. If Bev could not handle all the baggage that was going to accompany this endeavor, now was the time to bail.

David and Linda quietly floated in the private pool at their guest house retreat in Naples. The hosts were an architect and his wife who had completely renovated the 400 square foot guest house. The small galley kitchen was stocked with some essentials when they arrived – coffee, strawberries, bagels, yogurt and a mixture of nuts. The whole place was perfectly done for a couple to enjoy the outdoors whether they were inside or out. With windows on all sides, a screened in porch and a private pool and spa it had everything they needed. If all the shades were raised, it seemed as though the inside and the outside were one. The whole yard was theirs to enjoy with all the beautiful gardens, hammock and pond at the back of the yard. As evening approached, small twinkling lights came on around the porch and pool deck. Then spotlights shot up into the trees as evening crossed over into night. The soft pool lights made the idea of an evening swim inviting.

After arrival yesterday, they had enjoyed a walk along the beach (only 5 blocks from their rental) and a dinner at one of their favorite restaurants in downtown Naples. This afternoon, they would join Bev for an early dinner downtown and then meet with Paul at the gallery to see what some of his ideas were for the fundraiser.

David set his book aside and looked over at Linda.

"I just booked us a tee time on Pelican Bay Wednesday at 10:00. I know you said Bev did not want to play this time. This will give us a chance to further warm up our game since we have not swung a club in the last few months."

"That sounds good. Yes, Bev keeps her rounds to no more than two per week so we will play our second round with her. Do you think Paul would want to join us?"

"I asked him about it yesterday and it sounds like he is expecting a client to come in from New York sometime this week. He is not sure which day, but when he finds out, he may be able to join us. I think he is doing very well at the gallery. It has come a long way since he and Gwen first came down here 5 years ago. Paul gave me a booklet about the latest work they are doing when I saw him. Listen to this."

> *"We are a full-service gallery, satisfying every imaginable need arising from building and maintaining a fine art collection. We represent contemporary realism and traditional representational painting by premier international and American artists.*
>
> *Exhibiting Figurative, Landscape, Marine, still life, narrative, and abstract artworks. Ellsworth & Company has two other galleries; located on Lansbury Street in Boston, and Copper Street, Nantucket, MA."*

"According to Paul, they will be headed to Chicago next month for Uncle Norm's 90th birthday party so we will see them much sooner than usual. Gwen said she is hoping the weather does not get below 70 when they are there. Good luck with that in April!"

"You would never know she was born and raised in Chicago. She has become very warm-blooded – I guess that is what happens when you live in Florida." Linda glanced through the booklet to see what was new at Ellsworth & Company. Although she had recently read a couple of books on art, it was a subject she knew very little about. Bev and Linda had spent several afternoons at the Chicago Art Institute over the years and it had been very enjoyable. Little by little, Linda was learning how to look at art and something about the history of it.

"I'm going to take a dip." They headed out to the private pool and spent a lovely hour holding hands and drifting on separate rafts in the water. Unlike many couples, the more time David and Linda spent together, the better they got along. On vacations, they easily spent the days together enjoying the same activities, watching the same TV shows, reading books to relax, agreeing on what they wanted to do for meals. It was a relationship that involved few arguments and no compromises, no deals; they were completely on the same page without effort. At home, this made for a peaceful sanctuary where they could trust that they knew each other down to the core.

Finally, David dropped Linda's hand and paddled over to the side. "Let's have some a snack before we head downtown."

After a few hours wandering through the boutiques in downtown Naples, Linda, David and Bev walked over to the gallery where Paul greeted them warmly. Over the years, the cousins had become very close and they shared similar interests and political views. Linda and David lived by Gwen's father, so Gwen and Paul were most appreciative of having family to keep an eye on him.

"It's so good to see you guys. Bev, nice to see you again too – I remember a couple of years ago when you and Harry first visited us. We were so sorry to hear about Harry. How are you doing these days?"

"Well, I am gradually starting to get on with my life. There is always a lot going on at LF so there are many distractions. As you know Linda and I have a big project going with this fundraiser, so this is keeping me busy and it is such an important effort. We appreciate you being willing to support our fundraiser by holding an auction. This will be a good addition to our line-up of events that night."

"Yes," Linda said. It is no small feat to keep such a large group distracted for 24 hours. The auction will be an activity that will keep people awake and moving. It's a chance for you to develop some new clients and potentially sell some art as well."

"Some of the houses on LF are massive," David said. "They are not quite as big as some of the homes here in Naples, but there is a new section of homes that are all over 5000 square feet. Lots of space to include beautiful art."

"Well, should we take a look at some of the pieces I have and decide which would be best for the auction?" Paul led the way to the backroom where he stored all the art not currently on display in the gallery. There were painting, drawings, sculptures and even other 3D modern art pieces in every corner and hanging from the ceiling on moving racks.

"Linda, how much room is there and how many pieces do you think we will need?"

"I was thinking we would want to auction off at least 10 pieces. Perhaps we could plan it so that there are two periods to the auction each about 45 minutes long. Should we do it so that the least expensive pieces are first and then the auction builds drama as the prices go higher? I have been to silent auctions but have never seen how one is done live except in the movies."

"We could decide to display all the pieces first so that everyone can take their time and look at them. We might want to include as many as fifteen or twenty pieces to give more variety and so that more people might see something they like." Paul began to warm up as he described his ideas. "We can include all different sizes, but with twenty or so, there is a nice feeling of it being an art exhibit or a "gallery". So, the first part can be a viewing of the exhibit so people can see what will be in the auction."

"I like that idea," Bev said. "We can have champagne and hors d'oeurvres. There are some folks at LF that have refined taste and are interested in art so they would enjoy an art exhibit." We can make sure there is proper lighting to show off the pieces and set up displays that encourage people to wander through while they enjoy their refreshments.

"Then we will move on to the first half of the auction. With ten pieces, I think 45 minutes is a reasonable amount of time. That is roughly five minutes for each piece. It could take longer if we spent one or two minutes talking about the piece – like you would hear in an art gallery. This could be something brief about the artist, what is actually in the painting, - something that would help people who are not necessarily there to buy, but who want to know more about how to look at art."

"That is a perfect way to market the auction too – it is not only for buyers, but for anyone who is interested in knowing more about art. I like the idea of making it accessible and interesting for a large group of people," said Linda. "Would we also want to have people buy a ticket for a drawing to be held at the end of the first half?"

"Great idea, I have seen that done before and it also encourages more people to think of themselves as someone who is interested in art. It is another good way to include more people- some people can't resist a drawing where they might win something." Paul made a few notations on his iPad as they made decisions. They went on to look over his suggestions for the pieces to be included. With decisions made, the group headed out to the deck in front of the gallery to sit under the pergola.

"Paul, I think this has been so helpful and I can really see how the auction is going to work very well. We can't thank you enough for agreeing to participate in the fundraiser," said Linda. "Of course, you know the background and the motivation for this event. We think it is so important and it's a way for us to do something that could make a big difference. Sometimes I think about all this effort and I can't believe we are doing all of this. Then I listen to the news and remember it will all be worth it if we can pull this off."

"Gwen and I are so pleased that you thought of us and asked us to be a part of your plan. We may live here in Naples, but we are from Chicago, so our hearts are with you 100%."

"Now that we have gotten business out of the way, is anyone up for a walk on the beach?" David asked. They all headed down the block to the pier and view of the clear starry night.

Chapter 20 – May 2020

It was 5:30 AM and Bev's alarm was insistent on waking her up. Ignoring the too cheerful notes of Vivaldi emanating from her phone proved futile and Bev finally got up and pressed the dismiss button. One of these days she had to get one of those new alarm clocks that Linda had – the kind that made the room brighter like the sun coming up without any intrusive noise. Easier to ignore too, Bev thought grumpily.

Last night she had optimistically decided to get up early for a bike ride before the day got too hot. May in Florida was the beginning of those brutal summer months and most of the LF community took advantage of the cooler early morning hours to get in their daily exercise. Well, quite a few of the residents had fled back to the north, escaping the humidity and scorching temperatures. Those that stayed for the summer were mostly the retirees who were on limited budgets and couldn't afford a cabin in the Wisconsin woods or a cottage in Maine. Bev could have afforded to flee the heat and there was always the lovely guest house at Linda and Dave's, but this summer her task was to ensure that OL kept on track.

As she stumbled out the door to retrieve her bike she winced at the humidity. It would probably reach 90 degrees by early afternoon. Her head throbbed with the beginnings of a headache, but she climbed on her bike and headed down the street towards the bike trail. Several of her neighbors were loading up their golf carts with clubs and coolers, anxious to get in 18 holes before the day heated up and everyone would be relegated back into their air-conditioned homes. She waved to her neighbor Amy, who as usual over the past 6 months, ignored her.

Bev turned onto the trail, glad of the partially shaded path. Her headache eased up and she began to enjoy being out in the early morning. As her legs pumped faster and she built up some speed, her muzzy head entirely cleared. She knew it was the result of a bad night's sleep. She had tossed and turned all night, her mind churning with all the items still on the OL checklist.

The most pressing issue regarded her neighbor Amy, the one who snubbed her at every opportunity. Bev had learned that Amy was indeed planning to disrupt the fundraiser. Amy had been organizing a group of residents who had been meeting regularly throughout the winter and spring. Now, however, most of those had left Florida and wouldn't return until late September. Bev knew that many of them were avid Democrats but reluctant to participate in anything resembling a public protest. If she could take Amy out of the equation, Bev felt certain that the protest plan would just fade away. Bev laughed out loud thinking how Tom Clancy might arrange for a troublesome roadblock to be eliminated. But what, she mused, could she do? And it was not only Amy that was a problem.

Matt was running up against a very big potential complication with the Chief Information Security Officer at LF. Nelson Grimes was past retirement age from this position at LF, and a confirmed bachelor with no social life. He hung around Leisure Falls IT offices seven days a week, an officious self-appointed dictator of his small kingdom. While his younger staff members were perfectly capable of handling any issues, Grimes insisted that he have his hands in every project.

Matt had obtained a part-time position with the department which gave him access to both the software systems and hardware. This access would be invaluable for OL. However, Matt reported that Grimes practically lived in his office, and even when off duty, delighted in popping in unexpectedly at all hours, hoping to catch his staff slacking off. This was a big worry. Matt would need to access the data center and servers in the IT office during the long night of the fundraiser event; some of the software changes could be done remotely but others required Matt to physically manipulate the department's computers. Matt wasn't worried about the other staff members that would be on duty that night – they usually spent the always uneventful night shift napping or playing cards, rarely even glancing at the security footage or video feeds. But Grimes was a different story. His unpredictability made him a problem. If he decided to make a surprise inspection during the fundraiser and caught Matt in the act of making some significant alterations to the security software, the whole operation could be in jeopardy.

Bev spotted a bench ahead on the trail, a perfect spot to take a break and drink some of the iced tea in her insulated bottle. As she sat and enjoyed the cold beverage, she thought about the various friendships she had made at LF. While she had truly enjoyed Patricia's company all winter, it was a relief when she had left in early April, anxious to see the cherry blossoms that bloomed every spring in her old hometown of Washington DC. Patricia would be gone the entire summer, enjoying the season at her family estate in the Berkshires in upstate New York. Bev had given her a big hug goodbye, but she had been secretly elated to see Patricia leave LF, at least temporarily. Bev had recommitted to OL that night in Naples; she had decided firmly and resolutely that her loyalty to Linda as well as her conviction that Driscoll had to be denied a second term, were paramount in her life. She had returned from that trip knowing her remaining seven months at LF would be dedicated to this plan. But it was much, much, easier to do this without the complication of a budding friendship with a committee member. Bev would leave LF immediately after the fundraiser was over. If things went according to plan, (still a big IF) all of LF would know that Election Day had come and gone without their participation. Bev knew it wouldn't take long for accusations to be directed at her. Bev hoped with all her heart that she would then be many miles away.

Bev's thoughts then turned to her neighbor Amy. Amy was a small wiry gal with a deep Florida tan, happiest when whacking tennis balls or swimming laps in one of the community pools. She was a retired high school English teacher, living alone and frugally on a modest fixed income. Bev and Amy had originally bonded over their love of tennis and books, sharing both for several hours each week. But after Bev became involved with the fundraiser committee, Amy abruptly ended their friendship. Bev knew that Amy tended to hold on to a grudge. Amy could be a lot of fun to spend an afternoon with, but she could also be petty and judgmental. She was bitter about her small pension, jealous of those with the financial means to spend the summer in a cooler, more pleasant climate. Bev was certain Amy was seething that her plans to cause a disruption at the VFT event had to be shelved until her cadre of followers returned in the fall. By

124

then, Bev felt, the political frenzy that Amy had whipped up would have tapered off.

As Bev mounted her bike to make the return trip back to her house, she wondered if she could solve both problems –Grimes and Amy- with a single plan. If both Grimes and Amy were away from LF during the first week of November, there was a much better chance for OL to succeed. A lightbulb went off in Bev's brain and she jammed on her brakes. A cyclist veered around her, cursing at Bev but she did not even notice. A vacation, she thought. Even better, a free vacation. Rarely did either Grimes or Amy leave LF. Grimes because he had no interests outside of work and Amy due to her tight budget. But a free vacation, perhaps won in a raffle or contest, could remove both obstacles and Bev knew just the right vacation- a river cruise! Bev spotted another bench ahead. She called overseas to Mark, who was in the midst of organizing an afternoon walking tour of Passau Germany and told him her idea. Could he help? Mark promised to mull it over and call her later that day, after the onboard dinner service.

That day went slowly for Bev as she waited for Mark's return call. She had texted Mark throughout the day, giving him more details, explaining the potential obstacles that both Grimes and Amy posed. She tried to keep busy, facetiming with little Scotty and chatting with Ruthie about her new position at work. Bev was obviously distracted, which went unnoticed by Scotty but not by her daughter.

"Mom, what's up? You've asked me the same question three times."

"Lots going on with OL. Sometimes I feel overwhelmed with all the details. The next six months will be a whirlwind." Bev brought Ruthie up to date with all the problems and concerns. Bev was thrilled when Ruthie offered to come down to help.

"You know mom, this project is kinda crazy, but I support everything you are trying to do. My friends are pretty involved in their own lives-their careers, having babies, trying to buy their first house. They don't think about politics much but because of you, I'm talking to them about it. I'm really proud of you. And even though this is stressful, it's good to see you involved and passionate about something. You've been in a daze since Dad died. Jason, Ross and I have been worried these past two years. But now you seem alive again, engaged. I can't tell you how relieved I am, and I know Dad is looking down, happy to see you and Aunt Linda trying to fix the world, just like in your college days.

Just then Bev's phone beeped, indicating another call.

"Ruthie, I think it's Mark calling back. I'll tell you what he says tomorrow."

Bev disconnected from Ruthie and immediately recognized Mark's British accent over the line.

"Good evening Bev my girl. I'm a bit knackered, a long day with a boat full of boisterous Aussies but I have bloody good news."

Thirty minutes later, Bev said good night to Mark- it was now nearly midnight in Germany. Mark had really come through-he had solutions to both the Grimes and Amy problems. Mark had told her that getting Amy on a river cruise was easy. Viking management had been wanting to begin an aggressive marketing campaign in several of the mega retirement communities in the US. Viking was well aware that the demographics of these communities- upper middle class, well-educated retirees were just the clients Viking sought. And what better way to expand the Viking brand and promote customer loyalty then to offer a free all expenses paid cruise- offered, of course, during the first week of November. Mark was confident that Matt could arrange the E-raffle to select Amy as the big winner. Bev was equally confident that Amy would readily accept this luxury vacation, even if it meant missing the fundraiser. Bev had invited Amy to join her last August on the Danube River cruise and Amy had been bitterly disappointed when she couldn't afford to go.

As for Grimes, Mark had conjured up an ingenious solution, one that probably cost Mark more than a few favors. Mark had arranged for Grimes to receive an invitation from Viking to accompany a cybersecurity bootcamp cruise. The expert lecturer for the cruise will be Scott Schober, author of Hacked Again and CEO of BVS Inc., who is regularly interviewed by leading national publications and major network television.   Also, on the cruise will be Grahame Grieve, the FHIR (Fast Healthcare Interoperability Resources) product director at HL7. Grahame travels around the world giving lectures, guiding connectathons and advising governments and vendors about interoperability. He is on the list of *15 IT Standards and Interoperability Rockstars to Know*. This would certainly appeal to Grime's vanity; he would not be able to resist the opportunity to meet other cybersecurity experts. He would be invited to sit at the celebrity table for dinner, as well as receiving a private suite on the top-rated Viking Rurik, which cruised the Volga river between Moscow and St. Petersburg.

Bev couldn't stop smiling. Mark had solved her two biggest problems. An amazing contribution to OL, especially since he wasn't even an American citizen. She reached once again for her cell phone, anxious to share the news with Linda.

With the spring semester over, Linda was enjoying her favorite time of the year – summer. May and June were so beautiful, and she spent hours each day outside getting her garden planted for the season. This involved multiple trips to a variety of greenhouses and nurseries to select a few new perennials as well as several flats of annuals to add a pop of color. From experience, she had found that geraniums, begonias and marigolds with a border of sweet alyssum were low maintenance once she got them planted and they provided non-stop blooms and a garden that lasted well into the fall months. This week, now that there was no longer a chance for frost, Linda convinced David to accompany her to the final plant purchases of the year where she finished off the garden with sweet potato vine, red and gold coleus and her favorite - lantana.

Last week, she and David had taken a day trip to the Schlitz Audubon Center in Milwaukee to do some bird watching. This time, they saw redheads, ring-necked ducks and a half dozen different warbler species. They hiked the trails and climbed the 60-foot observation tower to view Lake Michigan above the tree canopy. The panoramic view of the shoreline to the big lake with the sun sparkling on the water reminded Linda of her mother's words – "focus on the beautiful things in life". At this time of year there was no shortage of the beautiful things outdoors.

Time was marching on toward the election too. The primaries had come to an end and the candidate for the Democrats, Governor James Butler of Ohio, had finally been chosen. His running mate would be decided at the convention being held in Milwaukee from July 13-16. Butler would be the person sparring with Driscoll over the next five months through the conventions and on into the fall as the country edged ever closer to November 3rd.

Linda was satisfied with the Democrat. He certainly was a good choice in terms of experience as an administrator. He was successfully running one of the largest states and had a strong record on enacting climate change policy and healthcare reform with a fiscally conservative budget. He also had a military background as a marine and was deployed to Afghanistan three times. What more could you want in a candidate? The other thing Linda really liked about Butler was his ability to dismiss the juvenile, bullying name-calling that left Driscoll looking like an incompetent fool. She only hoped he would be able to attract votes from millennials, independents and the critical Latino/African American groups. Once the debates began, everyone would see how well he handled the President's attacks and lack of substantive solutions to the many problems important to voters.

Tomorrow, on her call with Bev, they would review all preparations for OL. They had much of the program for the night in place. Thanks to the work Bev was doing with the fundraiser committee, the big contracts had been signed for the first musical performance by Rachel Stone and for Mark, the emcee for the night. They had finalized all the preparations for the art gallery and auction. As Linda roughed out the schedule for OL, she noticed a couple of gaps they would need to fill to make sure the attendees were busy and entertained throughout the night.

To add an element of fun, Bev had gotten the committee to approve the plan for guests to be wearing costumes of either dressy Monte Carlo casino-style for the women or country-western style for the men. The committee defined the costume contest guidelines and specified some restrictions (such as no weapons – even if your platform issue was gun policy). Undoubtedly there would be someone with bad taste and poor judgement who would push the limits on costumes, but then again, this would get everyone engaged and talking which was the overall goal. The fact that the election was right after Halloween meant that everyone would already have been thinking about costumes anyway so many would be able to get double use of their choice and not have to think up a new creative idea.

After reviewing the events, Linda thought they had one glaring hole they needed to address. Although the art gallery was a great idea, it would not appeal to everyone and they needed an alternative that would capture the interest of others. Since many of the LF residents loved to go to casinos occasionally, she thought a Monte Carlo night casino event would be perfect. This could start at 10:00 and go until 1:00 when the prize giveaways would be announced. This was a fun alternative and it was a good chance to involve lots of people as they set up different rooms for the various casino games. This would encourage movement from room to room and it would give them a chance to ensure that people were taking advantage of the O^2 bars they would make available.

With this additional item added, Linda drafted a rundown of the program and sent it to Bev in advance of their call. They would go over it in detail to finalize decisions on the events for the program and to make sure they could get everything ready.

Operation Lifesaver Program

- 7:30 – red carpet entrance (Mark commenting on the arrivals and costumes). This would be the time for guests to check their watches, phones and Fitbits so they could "unplug" and enjoy the evening.
- 9:00 EST (8:00 OL time) - The opening performance by Rachel Stone. Her high energy style and country western music would kick-off the event and keep the energy level high.
- 10:00 – Monte Carlo games open, slot machines, roulette, blackjack and craps tables
- 10:30 EST - Art gallery exhibit opens, champagne and hors d'oeurvres
- 11:00 EST – Auction of the first ten art pieces.
- Midnight – Art raffle drawing. The action continues and concludes at 1:00.
- 1:00 – casino prize giveaway – Grand Prize is two tickets to the inauguration, 2nd prize is a weekend trip to Miami, 3rd prize is new TV, 4th prize is choice from a group of prizes (eg: bottle of wine, new e-reader)
- 1:30 EST, Mark leads games and competition (singing competition –prizes given at 4:30)
- 2:30 – Fox News TV personalities Jesse Faulkner and his partner Amy Dean would hold a town hall style event that ends in a rally for the candidate.

- 3:30 – Enzo Valentino, Las Vegas/Sinatra style singer performance.
- 4:30 - Mark awards prizes for costumes and singing competition
- 5:30 breakfast is served.

The next day, Bev and Linda dialed in for their lunch call.

"This line-up for the program that you outlined really helps to see how it is all fitting together," Bev said. "It is going to be a busy night and we need to have it this way to keep everyone's enthusiasm and excitement at a high level."

"Yes, the more I looked at it, the more I saw there were still a couple of things we need to add to make the program cover the entire night. What do you think about the addition of a Monte Carlo style casino night?"

"This is a great idea; it is a high energy activity and people will love it."

"There are companies that specialize in hosting casino night fundraisers so we will hire one of them to take care of all the detail," Linda said. "I forwarded you a PDF of one brochure I found which gives us a list of all of their offerings so we can choose what we want to include. Is there someone on the planning committee who would be good to put in charge of overseeing the details once we get a contract signed?"

"This could be a good thing for Brad Summers to head up," Bev said. "He and his wife Katie go to casinos often. He is a conservative bettor, but he is always winning so he is very familiar with the games and how he would want to see things set up. I will contact him after our call today to ask him about it. Up until now, he has been faithfully attending the committee meetings, but he is quiet since Eric and Grimes suck up most of the oxygen in the room with their constant pontificating. The casino night is an activity where Brad can shine, and I think he is very confident on this subject and it will give him a key piece to be in charge of."

"Sounds like Brad is the right person to handle it and I see no reason why it would impact the need to keep the real purpose of the fundraiser secret." Linda said. "I had another thought that we should discuss. What do you think about having a professional photographer available throughout the night to capture the event? I think people would love to have pictures and since they won't have their phones to take selfies, maybe we should provide someone to take pictures. Usually this is done at fundraisers so they can post the pictures to social media. In our case, I don't think we will be doing that, but you never know what the benefit might be of having photos. We can upload the photos and run them throughout the night so people can see themselves having fun."

"I agree, we should have a couple of people taking photos that evening. People will expect to see that. We have some big performers showing up so it would be natural to capture shots of that as well as the costumes and competitions," Bev said as she glanced through the program events. "It's starting to sound like a lot of fun. I can see where I would like to be at this kind of event. We have had great ticket sales already – over 40,000 tickets sold, but when we start publicizing the details of the program, it will really boost more ticket sales."

"Yes, and I think this group will be very excited about seeing Jesse Faulkner and Amy Dean from Fox. That was the easiest phone call in the world – they couldn't wait to sign up for an appearance at the fundraiser. They will do a panel discussion for half an hour to do what they do best – talk craziness about the Democrats and lie about what Driscoll will do when elected again. Then they will shift to a rally where they will spur on the members of LF for Republicans to stir up the crowd. Another great way to keep the energy level high."

"If we follow that up with another signing performance, that should help us keep everyone awake and lead right into the contest winner announcements and breakfast. Then they will get the shock of their lives as they leave the fundraiser to find that it is already 7:00 pm, not morning."

"And we will have pulled it off!" Linda could picture their triumphant success.

"Well, it all looks good to me. I will follow-up with Brad."

"Ok, sounds good. I will send the program to Mark and to the Fox people so they all can see where they fit in. Have you booked your ticket to come up for your summer visit yet?"

"Yes, I booked it this morning. I can't wait to see the kids again and you know how much I love staying at your guest cottage. I will spend a wonderful six weeks with you and David at the lake. "

"We are so glad you are coming. I have just finished planting the garden so it will be all in full bloom when you get here. I can't wait to enjoy this time together before the final fall push. "

Chapter 22 – July 2020

July 5 dawned with a fiery crimson sky which was quickly replaced with charcoal thunderheads and before long a driving rain was soaking all LF. The main village square was a sodden mess. Debris from the Independence Day celebration littered the grounds, turning the usually well-manicured lawns into a quagmire of mud, soggy paper cups and used up roman candles, sparklers, and bottle caps. The festivities had gone late into the night, and the clean-up crews were only now beginning the massive job of returning the area to its normal pristine state.

Bev, huddled under an oversized golf umbrella, was on her way for morning coffee at Matt's rented condo, located on the far edges of LF. She kept her rain hat pulled low and the collar of her rain jacket up. The weather was doing her a favor. Only Edna and Miguel knew that she and Matt were siblings. As far as Bev knew (and hoped), no one else in LF knew of any connection between them and that's the way they needed to keep it. Usually, they kept their interactions to phone conversations, but Bev had a reason to see Matt face-to-face and the miserable weather afforded a great opportunity. Very few people were out in the downpour early on July 5. Those few that were out kept to themselves, intent on getting to a dry place quickly, and Bev was mostly concealed under her umbrella. She dared not park her bright blue golf cart in front of Matt's place – it was fairly recognizable – so she was hoofing it across the flooded streets.

Once dry, Bev sat at Matt's kitchen table, sipping her coffee and trying to ignore the plate of oatmeal cookies Matt had set out. They chatted easily about Bev's kids and Matt laughed uproariously over the exploits of little Scotty. Scotty had decided he needed a "stream of income" and was renting out his markers and crayons to his fellow students. Matt had given him an expensive set last Christmas, over 100 different colors, and the demand at Scotty's kindergarten class was high; Scotty was raking in quarters.

After finishing her second cup, Bev got down to the real reason for her visit. "Everything is going really well as far as OL. The committee is happy, our hourly events are shaping up and your team is doing marvelous work – I still can't believe Edna is such a computer whiz and who but my little brother would think to recruit a 6th grader. But I realize you are of course the master mind behind the whole operation. Without you Matt, Linda and I could never have gotten past the beginning steps. The IT aspect in manipulating the clocks as well as all the rest...I'm sure there is more stuff I don't even know about and couldn't understand anyway, and you just figured it all out. This crazy scheme won't work without you."

"Bev, it's OK, I know I'm appreciated"

"Let me finish Matt. I also know that you were perfectly happy up north, but you gave it all up to come to my aid. And I just totally love you for that. We haven't talked about what happens after the election."

"Well sis, I'm betting you're not planning on sticking around."

"But what about you Matt? I've dragged you down here and then I'm going to run away. I feel so guilty about that – like I just used you and now..."

"Bev", Matt broke in, giving his sister a long hug. "Bev, I am somehow happy here. It's completely inexplicable but I am. Years ago I tried to play the corporate game but I'm lousy at workplace politics. I did make plenty of dough and lucked into a few good investments and that enabled me to live a different, quieter life. I've lived alone my whole adult life and it's what I wanted. But this place has sort of grown on me. I like the fellas in Security and I just might be interested in running that department if we can dump Grimes. Lord knows it needs an overhaul."

"Won't the entire security department be blamed once it gets out what happened?"

No one in Security will be implicated—I've seen to that—and Grimes will be out of the picture, conveniently cruising down the Volga. And you know I have grown quite fond of Edna."

"You two aren't..."

"No, no, but I care about her, and I think maybe I've helped a bit with her mental fuzziness."

"Matt, I'm just flabbergasted."

"Frankly I am too. Maybe this relentless humidity has addled my brain but I'm content and I'm staying, at least for a while. I also have been thinking that by staying, I can control some of the backlash, maybe deflect any of the accusations heading your direction and keep you and Linda under the radar. My plan is to create so much misinformation that no one is sure what occurred and who was involved. Edna and I have lots of ideas how to make that happen."

139

A short time later, Bev slipped away seemingly unnoticed. Her mind was still trying to process all the extraordinary things Matt had said. She was so distracted she didn't notice the man across the street from Matt's. The man standing in the bay window, binoculars raised.

Chapter 23 – August 2020

At the end of another long summer day, he slowly walked the LF grounds. If anyone recognized him, they did not show it. Nobody asked what he was doing or took notice him. This made it very easy to check everything – he was the invisible man.

There were Mr. and Mrs. Helms heading toward the club for a late dinner. He entered the gate to the pool and saw the men's golf league casually lingering over one final drink before heading home to their wives. A few people were slowing gliding along the swim lanes relaxing after the hot summer day. It was all very predictable.

Below the surface though, he knew things were not business as usual. He had heard what the fundraiser committee was planning. With all the events that LF scheduled in a typical year, this alone did not particularly capture his attention. But he was good at keeping his eyes and ears open and his thoughts to himself. This practice had served him well in his life. It was all starting to add up and he knew what he would do.

Following the bike path around the 9th hole, he noticed a woman arriving home and pulling into her driveway. The garage door opened, and she got out of the car with her arms full of grocery bags. Why would she leave the car out in the driveway, he wondered? She left the doors to the car, garage and house open, apparently with no concern for safety. After all, this was a gated community and he was sure she believed that once inside the LF gates, she was safe. Most efforts to remind residents of basic safety guidelines fell on deaf ears and many people did not follow even the most basic precautions.

He had seen the same thing in the big cities – be aware of your surroundings, keep your cell phone stored and not out where it can be grabbed out of your hands. Most people did not listen. Now with Ring doorbells and other camera security, the proof was right in front of everyone and there was some shock at what was actually occurring where people had assumed they were safe. Crime could be anywhere. Those who naively thought otherwise sometimes learned that it could happen to them too.

A man with his beagle came down the path headed toward the dog park. This was an easy thing to do to have both companionship and a more secure home. Although he personally disliked dogs, any pet really, he thought it was a good idea for most residents. Aside from security cameras, dogs were a criminals' worst nightmare. Not having a dog of his own did not stop him from carrying dog treats everywhere he went on the LF property. They had come in handy many times for silencing a noisy pet.

Finally, he reached the community center where the inside was dark, except for the conference meeting room. Committee members were still seated around the table and the big screen was showing an overhead schematic of the big conference arena. He knew the fundraiser committee met on Wednesday nights and they often left evidence of what they were working on right on the table in plain sight or in the garbage after the meeting ended. He wandered over to the smoking area and took a seat at one of the tables to wait for the meeting to end. Just as he finished his cigarette, the lights in the conference room went out. Perfect timing.

He waited for the members to leave the building and caught the door just as it was slowly closing. Just as he suspected, he retrieved the meeting agenda from the table and scanned the items listed. So, they were inviting Fox News personalities to attend the fundraiser. He puzzled over this and thought about the other tidbits he had come across over the past several months. A fundraiser was a common event here at LF, but keeping his eyes open revealed that there was more going on. He was beginning to see what others were missing – not paying attention to the details right in front of them. If he was right, he would be ready to act. For now, though, he was going to keep watching and make his own plans.

. . . . . .

Bev and Linda relaxed while David grilled chicken and corn on the cob. It was a lovely summer evening at the lake, and they were enjoying the cooler evening after the heat of the day. Linda had prepared a bean salad to complement the meal and Bev had added some dark chocolates for dessert.

"The 90's in Chicago is so much better than 90's in Florida," Bev observed. "I know it is the humidity and all, but there is something else about it that seems full of possibilities."

"Well, I don't know if it is just the weather or if you are feeling confident about the Democrats' chance," Linda said. "The conventions always rev everyone up and make it seem that victory is surely ours. I have felt that before, so I don't trust it. Since they are only up in Milwaukee, I toyed with the idea of going up there to see what it is like to be where it

143

happens. Then I thought of how nice it would be to just stay here and watch it all on tv and without the driving and parking and walking … "

"I don't think we could have seen much if we had gone, our time is better spent watching and then polishing up our plans for OL."

"I'm sure you will enjoy my grilling more than anything you would have found in Milwaukee," David said. "Even if it is the Democrats, it is still a whole lot of hot air."

"True, I have very little confidence that they will be successful in making the changes they talk about. Healthcare – I have zero confidence that this will be solved before we reach Medicare. We are living with our fingers crossed that we make it to Medicare without a disaster. Unfortunately, I think they are willing to do something about climate change, but I don't think they can make much progress if elected. I guess I am getting pessimistic about a lot of this. All I want is to make sure we get that guy out of the White House."

Linda felt unsettled about the convention. Even with a strong candidate, they had an uphill climb ahead of them to get him elected. More than once, what should have been victory had been snatched away from the Democrats through sneaky tricks or, as some openly called it – cheating. David believed that "When you are playing the game, you must play to win." This made sense in the context of sports, did it also apply to politics? If the other side is willing to cheat to win, that makes it very difficult to maintain integrity. Should they do whatever it takes to win? Do the ends justify the means? How do you know when you have reached a crisis point that demands action that you previously would not have considered?

144

Over the years Linda had altered her thinking given the results of previous elections. It was naïve to believe that the right thing would eventually happen. She had given it time to play out and look where it had gone over the past 20 years. Looking back on the eight years Obama had been in office, she considered them to be a miracle and a brief respite from the general trend that was now apparent. She now wondered if what had looked to be progress and "the right thing", had ultimately unleashed a force that took the country down the wrong path, not toward progress, but down a very dangerous path that could end up in losing much more than just an election. What was the best way to deal with this serious threat?

"We have to stay the course and keep our efforts focused on the one thing we can do – Operation Lifesaver," Bev said. "This is the right thing to do. The closer we get to November, the more I am convinced of it. We have spent a lot of time planning and I am ready for the action to start."

Linda shook off her dark thoughts as she listened to Bev say what she was also thinking. "I'm with you 100% Bev. I can't wait to get this show on the road. Since we reviewed everything again today, was there anything that stood out to you that we need to work on?"

"One thing we can do is send out an update on the fundraiser in the next LF newsletter. We can emphasize the contests and share the plans for a casino night. I expect that will boost ticket sales to reach our goal," Bev said.

"Ok, tomorrow let's work on a draft of this for you to send to the committee for review so you can publish it when you get back in September.
"

Chapter 24 – September 2020

Bev drove South on I294 towards Chicago. After several weeks at Linda and Dave's home in Lake Geneva, it was time to make the rounds and see the kids. She and Linda had spent many productive mornings fine tuning OL and many lazy summer afternoons floating in the lake. Brad Summers had been excited about the casino idea and his enthusiasm had spread throughout the entire Victory for Driscoll committee. Brad was busy renting blackjack, craps tables and roulette wheels along with hiring dealers and croupiers. The casino idea had expanded to now encompass the entire second floor of the conference center and would also include poker tournaments. Between the casino, art auction, and musical entertainment, there was something for everyone. And Mark had devised many hours' worth of games and contests to keep everyone engaged.

Linda's idea of roving photographers was also received with enthusiasm. Bev's contribution was to suggest that Matt, an excellent amateur photographer, be unofficially added to the posse, thus giving him easy access to the entire convention center. Bev felt much more relaxed knowing Matt would be nearby for much of the evening. She knew that unexpected SNAFUs were likely to arise and having Matt there in the convention center, along with Linda and David, would increase the probability of success. Matt, Linda and David provided an enormous pool of smarts, problem-solving ability, and cool thinking under pressure, all of which would be needed in this colossal subterfuge. It was a foregone conclusion that the event would ostensibly be a great success as a

Republican fundraiser and tribute to Driscoll, but would be the underlying secret purpose of the event also be a triumph?

Bev was only a few exits from Ruthie and Ken's condo in Lincoln Park. The kids were making Bev her favorite dish, Cog Au Vin, a time-consuming casserole that involved many steps and dozens of ingredients. Bev enjoyed great meals, but she no longer had the energy or impetus to spend hours in the kitchen. Harry, thank goodness, had never been fussy about food and would cheerfully and uncomplainingly enjoy any odd mishmash that Bev had thrown together and called dinner. And Harry had consumed more than his share of frozen pizzas when Bev had been furiously working to make a magazine deadline. Harry had sure been a good husband, Bev thought for probably the ten-thousandth time. She was glad she had consented to uproot and move to Florida even if he had only been able to enjoy six months of sunny golf and poolside beers. She would never be able to forget that look of bewildered confusion when he realized he was having a heart attack. Fit, active, and sporting only the slightest of beer bellies, Harry had been an unlikely candidate for a life-ending cardiac arrest at age 63. Bev wondered what he would have thought of her involvement in OL. Harry had never been particularly involved in current politics; he had planned to fill his retirement by reading all his beloved detective stories. Authors like Robert Parker and John MacDonald had held his interest far more than CSPAN or Politico.

Bev rapped on Ruthie's door and was completely unprepared when little Scotty ran out and threw himself into her arms. After giving him many squeezes and kisses she peered into Ruthie's living room delighted to see her whole family assembled.

"Surprise Granny", squealed Scotty. "We are going to eat Aunt Ruthies Coggie with you".

Coq au Vin Scotty – Coggie sounds like breakfast cereal" Scotty's mom Debbie chuckled. She held a squirming baby Ella in her arms.

Bev immediately scooped up Ella, covering her plump cheeks with kisses. Bev had managed a few quick trips to Chicago since Ella's birth in February but her busy summer in Florida had kept her from her grandchildren for far too long.

"We thought we'd drive down from Wauconda to surprise you" Ross said. "Luckily, Ruthie made enough food to feed an army"

Bev looked around the room, beaming and filled with happiness.

After a wonderful meal, Ken volunteered to do the dishes while Debbie went on a mission to get Ella down for a nap. Jason suggested that the rest of them should go for a long walk through the neighborhood and let Scotty burn off a little energy. At least that was what Jason said was the reason for the walk. Bev had caught many glances exchanged between her three kids during lunch and she braced herself for an interrogation. Ross was the one who began.

"Mom, you look great and you seem pretty calm too – which is amazing considering what you have going on down in Florida. Ruthie has filled Jason and I in on the grand scheme. Debbie and I have...... concerns."

"Me too Mom," Jason interjected This seems pretty crazy. Could you get in any trouble over this?"

"Guys, Ken has asked his lawyer friends and Mom should be clear of any legal issues. While the clock manipulation at the event does flirt with voter suppression, there is likely not enough concrete evidence for anyone to get arrested. After all, they aren't locking the doors to keep people from leaving...you're not doing that right Mom?" Ruthie asked nervously.

"Of course not," Bev assured her. "We are just hosting a party that will be so much fun that no one will want to leave. At least, that's the plan."

"Ruthie, you're still planning on visiting Mom in October? You can talk to Uncle Matt when you're there? No disrespect Mom, but you don't always think everything through." Jason put his arm around Bev to soften his words.

Ruthie replied, "Yes and next month I'm having lunch with Aunt Linda when she comes down for her campus meetings."

"Gee whiz kids." Bev was beginning to feel ganged-up on as well as a bit patronized. "You don't have to run to Matt or Linda for information...I'm not a child.... or an idiot. Linda and I have spent hundreds of hours planning this. It has a good shot at working and if it doesn't and the LF community ends up getting to the polls, then at least I'll know we tried our best. It's better than doing nothing, better than just sitting around complaining about how terrible Driscoll is." Bev was beginning to feel very hurt and angry at her kids.

"Mom, Mom, we just love you and we know how lost you've been since Dad died. We're glad you have something big to work on and we're terribly proud that you want to make a real difference. Hell, you're an actual revolutionary just like those guys in the play Hamilton – "not

150

throwing away my shot". You can't get upset because we worry about you." Ross tried to sooth Bev's hurt feelings. "Now fill us in with all the activities that are going to keep those Florida oldsters busy all night."

Bev, only partly mollified, began to describe the planned events as they slowly ambled up and down the streets of Lincoln Park.

Later that day, after Ross, Debbie, and the kids headed back to the suburbs and Jason left to get ready for a summer evening sailboat cruise on Lake Michigan with his friends, Bev, Ruthie, and Ken sat on Ruthie's deck and watched the sunset. Bev was still feeling a little defensive. She didn't absolutely need her children's blessing but knowing she had their support would help to relieve her growing anxiety. After all, the election and OL was only 3-1/2 months away.

Ruthie bought out her special Southside cocktail – Gin with lots of tart citrus, and a platter of antipasto – cheeses, olives, pickled veggies and prosciutto. She reached over and gave her mom a long hug and said, as if reading Bev's mind, "Mom, we all believe in you. You have our unending support. You can't be mad if we worry – you are..."

Bev's phone started buzzing. She tried to ignore it, but text messages started appearing, all from Brad Summers. Bev gave Ruthie an apologetic shrug and answered the next call.

"Brad – What's up?"

"Bev, we have a problem. I'm sorry to bother you. I know that you are in Chicago with your kids, but this can't wait. As the committee head, Eric investigated our insurance policy for the conference center and having a casino somehow increases our potential liability – we need an additional security team just for the casino area. I talked to Grimes and he said the LF team can't handle it. His men are not contracted to deal with security issues inside the center. I looked into hiring an outside group, but none are available – they are all busy with election events throughout the state. Eric suggested we just cancel the casino but...we can't. I did something that was perhaps foolish. To get the best price possible I had to pay the whole rental fee upfront, with a no- cancellation policy."

"Brad, that wasn't what the board agreed to."

"I know Bev, but Eric was on my back about costs and this seemed like a great solution, 30% off rental price. But now we're committed – we can't get our money back and besides the casino has really boosted sales. I'm panicking here Bev – Patricia's gonna kill me when she finds out."

"Let me think Brad." Bev could feel Ruthie's eyes on her as well as her blood pressure rising. "I'll call you back."

Bev hung up and took a big swallow of her drink. Ken and Ruthie listened intently as Bev filled them in with this latest glitch.

"How bad would it be without the casino?" Ken asked.

"Pretty bad – we'd be out a boatload of money plus we've had a surge in ticket sales due to the promise of a casino as part of the event. It would be at the very least, awkward and embarrassing to cancel it."

Ruthie had been very quiet since Brad's call. Bev had just assumed that Ruthie was newly convinced that her Mom's big project was tearing apart at the seams. But Bev was wrong; Ruthie was committed to her Mom's success and had been casting about for a solution.

"Mom, didn't you and Aunt Linda host a casino night at your sorority? I remember you telling me about it. Didn't it end in a big fistfight between some fraternity idiots and the guys you had for security – weren't the security guys Uncle David and all of his friends from his old neighborhood?"

"Yeah, that's right. David's friends were a tough lot – they made sure no one cheated or left the building carrying out beers." Bev chuckled at the memory. "And yes, when a few drunken frat boys were about to wreck the whole thing, they very quickly took care of it. There were a few broken noses that night, but none were from David's group."

"Is it possible that they could do the same thing for your casino night – maybe without any fist fights this time?"

"It's a pretty crazy idea but then again this whole event is getting pretty crazy. I don't know..."

"Call Aunt Linda, Mom. I bet she can convince Uncle David to do it. And how great would it be if you, Aunt Linda, and Uncle Matt had your own security team around – I know we'd all be feeling lots happier about things if we knew you had some backup of your own. If anything goes majorly wrong and things get scary for you guys, Uncle David's friends would be right there, breaking a few noses if needed."

The next morning, Bev made the call to Linda. After looking at the casino problem from every angle, Linda agreed to talk it over with David.

She couldn't make any guarantees – David and his friends had all moved on from those college days. They had married, had kids and were preparing to retire. But they remained a tight group – they had played softball together for 30 years in a 16-inch league and now that they were older and slower, met for weekly golf. It was a possibility that they just might do this. Linda promised that by the time Bev drove back up to Lake Geneva the following week, she would have an answer.

Chapter 25 – October 2020

Meet the 71-year-old staging a one-man protest in his Trump-loving retirement community

Ed McGinty is a rare protester in the Trump stronghold of The Villages. "When Trump won, it changed the whole ballgame for me," McGinty says. "I thought to myself, 'This was supposed to be a joke. What's wrong with these people?'"

In the three years since then, the once-quiet political observer has transformed into the best-known Trump protester in The Villages, …McGinty's daily vigil with signs blasting the president as a "Sexual Predator" (among other things) has drawn ire in the Trump-loving Florida town he has called home since 2016. It has also brought viral fame.

"I'm proud that I'm standing up for what's right," he said. "There's never been a doubt in my mind that what I'm doing is right."

Brittany Shammas, *Washington Post*, Feb. 8, 2020

Linda prepared for her long commute. The sky was no longer light in the morning when her alarm went off, and soon it would be dark as her train headed into the city. Luckily, the chill of fall had not yet hit, and she was still able to wear a light jacket and feel comfortable.

She felt confident that they were prepared for Operation Lifesaver. One additional piece of the plan would hopefully be in place after David's golf league tonight. The need for security for the casino room had prompted him to raise the question with several of his friends.

David's friends had all lived their whole lives in Chicago – not more than ten miles from their childhood homes and the high school from which they had all graduated. At first, when Linda pitched the idea, David thought the guys would have no interest. But after the golf league round on Tuesday, the guys gathered in the clubhouse for a beer and he raised the question – would they be willing to reprise their role as security at a Linda and Bev sponsored event?

David held his breath waiting for their reaction. As he looked around the table, he saw that they thought he was out of his mind.

"Sure, we'll be security for you," Joey said. "I'll bring my brass knuckles just to keep everyone in line."

"Right," Mike added smiling, "They'll all listen to a bunch of old guys with glasses, bad shoulders and knee replacements." "Come on Zuey! Get serious". They all laughed. Zuey was the nickname they all had for David going back 50 years. It was something to do with a Zulu warrior, hard to remember the exact connection all these years later, but the name still stuck.

" Everyone in the place will be old, Mike. That's what makes this easy," David explained. "Free alcohol all night and all you have to do is look like security. This meets the requirement for them to have the casino night."

"Wait a minute, how many single women will be there?" JJ asked. "Meeting women on these dating apps is driving me crazy. I come across much better in a personal situation. If there are single women involved, count me in."

They all laughed again knowing how JJ was always in search of a new woman. The truth was, he was a good guy, but lonely after his divorce. He was a salesman at the core, and they knew his sharp wit and sense of humor were also a strong attraction for women, and at 6'2", with a slender build, blue eyes and a full head of wavy blond hair he was certainly easy on the eyes.

"What about Bobby?" Joey asked. "If I recall, he was the one who shut that smart guy up last time we were security."

"Yeah, that was a quick reaction I think." David was walking a fine line between getting them interested, but not having this become too big of a deal. "There will be no call for getting physical at this event."

"Well, as I recall, the guy asked for it and Bobby was just doing what he was supposed to do. No harm, no foul," Joey said.

"Actually, the guy had to have surgery, but whatever, he was fine." Mike dismissed the issue.

"This time it would be just a fun night out together for us, free liquor, many single ladies for JJ – what else do you want?" David made a convincing case. "I actually called Bobby yesterday to see if he would do it. He is only two hours south of there. Living the good life, renting bikes on the beach. What a life huh? Bobby thought it was hysterical when I told him. He said the last thing he ever wants to do was end up living in a place like that with all old people. Have you ever seen his place down there? He may be renting bikes, but his house is beautiful with a horizon swimming pool and a view of the gulf. All that work at the board of trade really paid off for him."

"Ok, you convinced me. I'm in. We can go back to Bobby's place afterward for a long weekend. When do we go and what do we need to do?" Mike was warming up to the idea.

"I will plan this out as a golf trip. We leave on Sunday, November 1. We'll play a quick round when we get there. Play another 18 on Monday. Then get the lay of the land from Linda and Bev. The event is on Monday night. There have already been 35,000 tickets sold so they are expecting a huge crowd. There are several other performances and events going on throughout the night, but all we have to worry about is the casino room."

"We will spend our time in the casino area and will make rounds in teams every 30 minutes. So, you will have 15 minutes on to round and then the rest of the hour just keep your eyes open for any kind of trouble. It is a charity event supporting the inauguration of Driscoll, so everyone is probably going to be in a real good mood and celebrating before election day. We'll stay until the end of the event and then head down to Bobby's house for a visit. "

"Sounds like a plan. I'll have my bags packed and ready to go," said JJ.

"Thanks guys, this will really help Linda and Bev. Having the casino night is crucial for attracting ticket sales," David said.

"That's us, nothing but helpful," Joey said with his arms stretched wide to demonstrate how open he was to the plan.

Later, David pulled into the driveway and brought his clubs into the house to clean. Linda and Wilson were on the couch in the den relaxing and watching a movie.

"I didn't expect to see you up when I got home," David said. "Now I can deliver the good news. I pitched the idea to the guys and with a little convincing, they agreed and are officially on board for Operation Lifesaver."

"That is excellent news! This is one less thing for us to worry about. I will text Bev so she can update Brad who will be very relieved."

"I actually feel a lot better about having them there with us as the evening unfolds," David said. "We don't know what may come up unexpectedly and we will need to be able to solve problems that arise quickly. I don't know what it will be, but something will happen that we are not expecting so we can rely on the guys to have our backs. One thing is for sure, I can count on them."

"I feel better about it too. As we get closer to the day, I would not say that I am worried, but I do feel some anxiety about how it will all go. We have planned and prepared, but it is like hosting a major party and you want it to go well. In this case, we want it to be successful in keeping people so occupied that they don't pay close attention to the day and time, ultimately keeping them out of the voting booths."

Linda got up and stretched, looking at her Fitbit to see the number of steps she had for the day. Another goal reached; it really was not asking too much to get 8,000 steps per day. With Wilson and David, who both liked taking walks, it was no problem. Their walks were more than just good exercise though, it was a time for them to connect, to talk about the details of the day without interruption, without the TV and without phones. Linda enjoyed being outside, and when they moved to the lake, she realized that it was exactly what she needed to be connected to nature in her life every day.

She thought again about November 2 and all that was riding on Operation Lifesaver. She and Bev had taken on big plans before, but nothing on this big of a scale. She thought about all the people that had become involved – both those that knew the whole plan and those that did not. Many friends and neighbors were pitching in just to be in on a fun event and they had no idea of the significance of what they were doing. More than ever, Linda was convinced that they were doing the right thing. Now the ball was rolling, there was no turning back, the momentum was building as November 2 approached. They were ready to let the party begin.

Chapter 26 – October 2020

Bev pulled up to the arrivals at Orlando Airport, excited to pick up Ruthie. She had a small cooler in the back seat filled with icy cans of Perrier and sliced mango. Her house was stocked and ready for a visit from her lovely accomplished daughter. In fact, Bev had hired a cleaning crew so that everything would be "Ruthie-clean", a term she and the boys used to indicate a higher level of sparkling cleanliness and order that a visit from Ruthie required. Ruthie would never ever be rude or disdainful, but Bev had always felt that Ruthie viewed her housekeeping as a bit slapdash.

Bev spotted her daughter through the crowds. Bev and Harry had always thought there was a special glow to Ruthie, an inner light that made her stand out and shine in a crowd. Yes, with her slim athletic figure, lemony blond hair and green eyes she was definitely attractive, but it was her kindness, intelligence and compassion that gave her something extra – something that drew people towards her like a beacon on a dark night.

"Ruthie, over here," Bev called out.

Ruthie hurried over with a smart carry-on in tow, balancing an unwieldly package in her arms, which turned out to be a tub of Garrets popcorn – half caramel, half cheddar cheese. Garrets was a Chicago classic and Bev and Ruthie had consumed many a bucket while watching the old Bette Davis movies that Bev loved.

"What a grand treat," Bev exclaimed.

"Good thing it fit in the overhead compartment. If it had been in my lap it would be half gone by now."

Bev navigated her way out of the airport and headed west towards home. She and Ruthie chatted about Ruthie's job in Chicago and all the latest news regarding Operation Lifesaver. Before long they were home, fixing a light lunch of chicken salad and fruit.

"Ruthie, I hope you don't mind a few hours on your own. The last committee meeting is at 2:00 PM today."

"No big deal. I'll sit out on the patio and soak up some Florida sunshine. It's been rainy and chilly in Chicago for the past four days. I need to check some work emails anyway."

"Ruthie, you are only here for the weekend – you can't just forget about work?"

"Well mom I have a surprise for you...I put in a request to work remotely from here for the next ten days. I want to be here for the event. I can help you and Aunt Linda and make sure you get out safely. I even bought a dress that's perfect for the Monte Carlo theme – I found it at a great vintage shop in Logan Square. Is that OK?"

Bev wrapped her daughter in a big hug "It's more than OK – it's the very best news."

Several hours later Bev returned from the meeting. She started filling Ruthie in on all the committee discussions, but it was obvious Ruthie was distracted.

"Ruthie – what's wrong? Is there a problem with work?"

"No, everything is fine in Chicago. It's a slow time there which made this trip easy to extend. No, it's not about work. It's something that happened here while you were gone."

Ruthie went on to describe how a car marked as LF security kept driving slowly past the house. She couldn't clearly see the occupant through the tinted windows except that it looked like a slim man with dark hair, maybe in his 40s.

"Is this normal Mom? I don't remember noticing something like this during any past visits. Am I feeling paranoid?"

"I think we are both a bit jumpy – I saw something on the way home that seemed odd too. You remember Edna, right? She's helping Uncle Matt with some of the IT issues. She knows parts of our plan for the fundraiser but not the whole story. Anyway, she was talking with Miguel's dad and something about it just bothered me. Hey, it was probably his car you saw – he is one of the fellas at the main gate, but I have never seen him patrolling the neighborhoods. It's probably nothing – maybe he was filling in for some patrolman out sick or something." Bev thought about it for a while and decided to just leave it for now.

"Maybe we should call Linda and tell her the good news about your staying."

Ruthie blushed and stammered "Actually, she already knows Mom. We had lunch in August, and I asked her what she thought of my being here to help. But I didn't know until last week that I could really make it work. I wasn't deliberately keeping it from you – I just didn't want you to count on it and then be disappointed."

Bev swallowed a few hurt feelings at being left out of the loop. She had always encouraged the close relationship between her best friend and daughter. In fact, Ruthie and Linda shared many traits, almost as if Ruthie had inherited a portion of Linda's genes through some kind of best friend pregnancy osmosis. Ruthie's organizational skills and driving self-motivation mirrored Linda's down to a tee. Ruthie even followed Linda's career path into the public health arena. Bev had never been jealous of their bond and she decided this was not the time to start. After all, this project would need all the skilled help it could get, and Ruthie would be invaluable – at the very least her youthfulness would ensure that at least one member of the OL team would be up to battling the fatigue of the 24-hour event.

"I'm just thrilled you're staying Ruthie – want to go out for sushi tonight?

Over tuna tataki and vegetable tempura, Bev bought Ruthie up to date on all the aspects of OL. She told her about Amy and Grimes and the Viking cruises that Mark had arranged for them. As Bev had anticipated, Amy's group of would-be protesters returned to LF in the fall with much less motivation to upset the Victory for Driscoll event and any remnant of political unrest faded away once it was known that Amy wouldn't even be in the country during the election. Ruthie thought it was ironic that Bev's success with OL was tied to the success of the Republican fundraiser.

"My friends back home would find it hilarious that I was in Florida helping my mom give a bash honoring Driscoll. He is absolutely despised in Chicago. Now tell me more about Mark."

"Well he's arriving next week Saturday. You will like him – he's personable and charismatic – a perfect Master of Ceremonies. He's used to handling large groups of inebriated geriatrics. Mark keeps things fun and lively but doesn't allow a party to get out of hand, and most importantly, he is used to handling unpredictable situations. You are good at that too, Ruthie. Did I tell you how happy I am to have you here?" Bev smiled fondly at her daughter as she poured the remaining sake into their cups.

The pieces were falling into place. Bev would call Linda tomorrow and give her the details of the final committee meeting. In just ten days the two events would run simultaneously: the Victory for Driscoll fundraiser and Operation Lifesaver. If both succeeded, Bev and Linda's plan to influence a presidential election might just be accomplished.

Chapter 27 – October 2020

Cyberwar to Kinetic War: 2020 Election and the Possibility of Cyber-Attack on Critical Infrastructure on the United States

"It would be comforting to report that those agencies charged with responding to disaster are adequately prepared to deal with the consequences of a cyberattack on the grid. They are not. The Department of Homeland Security has no plans beyond those designed to deal with the aftermath of natural disasters".

Jonathon Lancelot, *Small Wars Journal*, 29 Jan. 2020

"Hi Bev." Linda adjusted the monitor as she logged on to their last lunch call before she met Bev in Florida.

"Hi, just getting my notes from the last committee meeting. We went over the entire schedule of events and it looks like everything is ready to go."

"Good, I would like to go over that too. Did anything come up as a red flag, something that we need to take care of? "

"Not really. Grimes was talking about cybersecurity related to the election. He believes there will be some kind of attack or maybe even a series of attacks by the Russians prior to the election. He gave us an article talking about the Homeland Security's Cybersecurity Infrastructure Security Agency and how they have been taking all necessary precautions to thwart such attacks before and after the elections." Bev held the article up for Linda to see. "It says here that they think databases could be targeted by ransomware, and then encrypted making it unreadable until the victim pays the attacker–usually in cryptocurrencies such as Bitcoins. "

"I'm glad to see Grimes taking this so seriously. I know he's an odd duck, but I think it's possible he's way more adept at his job than you and Matt realize. I do think we might see that others are also doing their best to interfere with the election. It's important for us to remember that those plans could impact our plans and lead to some unexpected outcomes." Linda thought about this and took a bite of her chicken salad sandwich. My flight arrives Tuesday, which gives us almost a week to get the last-minute things done."

"I will begin to relax when I see Grimes go off on his cybersecurity cruise. He was starting to talk about how he regrets missing the fundraiser after all the work he has done for it. He is conflicted about it though because he really does want to meet all the cybersecurity experts from around the world. He will go because it is just too great of a deal to pass up." Bev seemed to take a deep breath but did not add anything more.

"Is there something else on your mind that we should discuss? What is the number one thing on your mind, what is keeping you up at night?" Linda asked.

"There was one thing I wanted to mention to you. It is probably nothing, but after our committee meeting, on the way home I noticed that Edna was walking with Jose Martinez, Miguel's dad. They seemed to be having a very intense conversation, which is unusual for Edna. "

"Do you think Edna knows more than we think she does? She has a lot of capability and it would be easy to underestimate her."

"Well, we have not included her in all of our plans, but I think she is putting two and two together and has some idea that there may be more to this fundraiser than meets the eye. I'm not saying she knows everything, but I think she has guessed some things. I don't know what she could have been talking about with Jose, but Miguel is pretty involved, and he may have said some things at home that got Jose thinking. I have seen him lingering in the smoking area by the pool, which is right across from the conference room we use for the committee meetings. Maybe it's nothing but seeing them together talking like that made me start to wonder."

"You may be right, there could be something going on there. We should take care to keep in close touch with Edna, Jose and Miguel as we get closer to the fundraiser. We need to keep an eye on all of them and see if they know more than we think they do. We don't want them to go "rogue" on us and do something we are not expecting." Linda leaned back and gazed up at the ceiling thinking. "Why don't we schedule lunch with Edna when I get there? I met her once before, but I would like a chance to get to know her better. This could build her confidence in us too – even if she doesn't know exactly what we are doing, she will still be supportive."

"Ok, that is a great idea. I will set up lunch with Edna for Wednesday." Bev scribbled a to do note on her calendar. "To go along with that, what do you think about this idea - I have another tutoring session with Miguel set up for Tuesday. Maybe I will ask him if his parents would want to talk about plans for him enrolling in a coding boot camp over the winter school break.dd"

Bev got out her calendar and paged through to the next week. "If you are here, we could both talk with them and you can endorse the idea as a university professor. We should look up some programs that are available and be able to talk specifics. They don't have a lot of extra money for something like this, so we could talk about a scholarship for Miguel to be in the boot camp."

"Yes, we should do that – both to keep an eye on them for the fundraiser, but also because we really do want to make sure Miguel gets some opportunities. He is a smart young man and seems to naturally take to computer work but with some extra focus, he could be on a great track for success as a computer engineer. We should talk with Matt and get his ideas on this too since Miguel looks up to him so much." Linda drained her iced tea and polished off the last bite of her oatmeal chocolate chip cookie.

"Ok, I think these steps will help us to stay in touch with some of the key people on our team. We need their help for this to work, whether they know it or not."

"Let's review the schedule again and make sure we have not forgotten anything."

They spent the next 15 minutes looking through the line-up for the fundraiser. As the emcee, Mark would arrive on Saturday and begin to familiarize himself with the layout, the timing of events and would shop for prizes for the best costumes. He had suggested that the event call for men to arrive dressed in something with a country western theme. The women would dress as something related to Monte Carlo casino games. This would give Mark the time he needed to get into character for his important role in keeping the evening moving along. They would also introduce him to the committee members and all the key people working on the fundraiser.

They also discussed their plans for escape as Operation Lifesaver ended. Bev, with Matt's help had gradually started to move boxes out of her house and into a storage facility she rented in Fort Meyers. She had made arrangements for Matt to move into her house so the remaining furnishings could stay as they were. Everything meaningful to her had been moved out and even though it was still her house, she felt like she was camping out in it – in limbo. Bev wanted to be able to just walk away that night and never come back. She would be sad to leave in some ways, but she was glad Matt would have the house now and as she had been planning this event, she became more and more ready to move on with her life.

After leaving the fundraiser at 6:00 am, Linda, David and Bev would drive directly to the Fort Meyers airport. They would fly back to Chicago and expected to make it back to the lake house by noon. It would be November 3rd and it would be over. They would know if their plans had succeeded and if they had made a difference.

Linda had begun to pack for her trip and would finalize everything on Monday night before her flight. Bev would pick her up at the airport at 3:00 pm on Tuesday. Then they would have five days to work out any remaining kinks in the plan. Linda thought about all the people out there that were planning to vote soon. Even with the dismal job done by Driscoll, 50% of the voters thought he was doing a good job. Nothing was in the bag at this point even though most polls placed Governor Butler six points ahead of Driscoll. Butler had done his part to get to the election without getting derailed by efforts to make him look weak to the voters. Would he be able to pull it off?

Linda remembered four years ago when they thought they would elect the first woman President of the United States. They could take nothing for granted. It was not over until it was over that night and they still had a big job to do to play their part.

Mark gave his red satin bowtie a final adjustment and used the full-length mirror in his hotel room to run through his usual pre-event checklist. The new Versace tux was a very classy addition to his already ample collection of tuxes and dinner jackets. For most, tuxedos were an item to be rented or perhaps purchased as a once in a lifetime splurge. But for Mark, eveningwear was a basic component of his working life, almost a uniform. He ran a practiced eye over his reflection, from his freshly polished made-to-order Italian shoes to the new rinse he had the hotel salon apply to his hair to allow just a hint of gray at his temples.

No one but himself would ever realize the effort and expense that went into transforming a working-class ruffian from Manchester into this sophisticated man about town. But he had learned as he had scraped and fought his way up the cruise ship food chain that appearance and affability were paramount. There were only a few Viking old timers that would remember the ill- mannered belligerent 17-year-old that had started in the kitchen as the night shift dishwasher. His slow but steady rise through the ranks had never been easy and he had given up any semblance of a personal life to attain the position of cruise director.

Over those years he had shed the chip on his shoulder towards those with more money, education, or opportunities. He had forced himself to return to school, spending long hours learning the hospitality business. Mark then deliberately remade himself, collecting those personality traits that would lead to success. He had even hired a retired actor to transform his crass Manchester accent into the upper-class tones of an Eton alum.

Now at the pinnacle of his career, he felt restless and this latest gig was just the anecdote. It had amused him when Linda had called, laying out the plan for the event, but he surprised himself when he agreed to be master of ceremonies. Mark had very quickly realized all that Bev and Linda were attempting. Although he would gain little monetary compensation, his working-class roots delighted in helping to usurp a leader who achieved power and money at the expense of the blue-collar workers he was disingenuously professing to help. Mark gave himself a wink in the mirror and happily anticipated a long but lively night. Americans were so easy to impress.

* * * * *

Howie Walker grumbled all the way to the Conference Center: the tickets were ridiculously expensive, he was missing Monday Night Football, and most of all, these new cowboy boots were much too tight. His toes felt in the grip of some cruel vise; he never should have bought them. But Marcy had insisted he follow the suggested recommendations of western wear for the guys, so he had gone over to the Shoe Depot and found these on clearance, only half a size smaller than his normal size. Mistake, mistake. This whole night was a mistake.

Howie and Marcy weren't fancy dress up types. Married for 43 years, most of it spent in a small bungalow outside of Council Bluffs, Iowa, he and Marcy had raised three kids together. His job selling tires at the local Sears had provided an adequate living. The boys had always had the sports equipment they needed, even if most of it had been slightly used. When Marcy started working part time at the Super Saver, things had eased up and they started putting a bit aside for retirement. They had spent many an icy winter night dreaming of a carefree life in Florida as a reward for all those austere years. And here they were.

Howie glanced over at Marcy and his gaze softened. He knew Marcy was worried that her bright fuchsia gown, also bought on the clearance rack, would look cheap next to their neighbors' extravagantly sequined garments purchased at boutiques in Naples and Bonita Springs. They pulled into a parking spot and Howie jumped out. He rushed to open the passenger door, surprising Marcy with a courtly dip of his cowboy hat and a big smack on the lips. Marcie giggled, reminding him of the young brown eyed girl he had clumsily proposed to all those years ago. Suddenly the shoes weren't quite so tight after all.

* * * * *

The Conference Center was awash in light. Spotlights were positioned all along the red carpet as couples poured in, all over 60 and all dressed to the nines. It was obvious that many of the men felt awkward in their unfamiliar cowboy garb, pulling on the string ties and adjusting their shiny silver belt buckles. The Orlando Western Wear and Saddle Shop had virtually sold out of their inventory of cowboy snap shirts and the red carpet was a sea of wannabe Marlboro men, looking as if they were attending a rodeo filled with bull riding and calf roping. In an almost jarring contrast, the women were elegantly be-gowned, coifed with sweeping updo's. The only concession to age was the preponderance of flats beneath the shimmering floor-length evening dresses. Some of the younger gals, those closer to 60, chose shorter cocktail dresses, showing off legs toned and tanned from countless hours on the links or tennis courts. As the couples neared the entrance, they could hear Mark extolling in his very upper crust British accent, "All cell phones and watches will be left in the coat room. Let the world fall away."

* * * * *

Miguel and Edna peeked through the curtain of the coat room. Although their task was to label and shelve the cell phones and wristwatches which were being collected at the main entrance, they found time to gape and giggle at all the cowboys and glamorous ladies bursting into the central lobby. While they were technically neither patrons nor staff, they had both dressed up in honor of the occasion -- Miguel in a sky-blue tuxedo he had worn to his cousin's wedding and Edna in an olive-green macramé dress, many years old but still serviceable. In fact, with her long gray hair bound in a French braid, she looked very elegant in a retro kind of way. Her eyes sparkled with both excitement and clarity. She knew that Bev and Linda thought she was too muddled to understand the extent of their plans, but they were wrong. Edna had been listening very carefully all along. She knew everything about Operation Lifesaver, and she was determined to look for an opportunity to contribute. She had even enlisted some outside help.

* * * * *

Tall, with auburn hair and still stunning at 56 in her emerald silk gown, Lily Barton checked the contents of her purse once again. The 80 five-hundred-dollar bills were still securely stowed in her jeweled money clip, her lucky money clip--the one she had brought to the casino in Baden-Baden those many years ago. That was the night she had struck it big playing roulette. A night to remember. The night that had started her on a path of rolling the big wooden wheel of Lady Luck in every casino throughout Germany, France, and Monte Carlo.

For one entire season her luck had held, and she had parlayed it into a small fortune, enough to set her up with a clothing boutique in Palm Beach. All those years building her business into a shop that catered to women like Columba Bush and Ivanka Trump. The always elegant Ms. Barton exuded taste and luxury, and few would ever guess that her years before the trip to Europe were spent re-shelving jeans and T shirts at the Old Navy in Pittsburgh.

That trip to Europe had been truly charmed and Lily had been smart enough to know that lightning doesn't strike twice. She had never set foot in a casino since their return to the states--hadn't even gambled on a lottery ticket. Until tonight. Tonight, she needed a seriously ridiculous blaze of good luck.

Long ago, Lily had set aside a small portion of her winnings for a rainy day--the amount now secreted in her purse. As savvy as Lily was at business, her judgment in choosing men was dismal. Time and time again she chose men who were deceitful, duplicitous, and often just plain mean. Her friends called them fixer uppers--losers whose potential only Lily saw--erroneously as it happened--over and over again. This last one, Simon, had nearly cleaned her out, and she was too embarrassed by her appalling lack of judgment to reach out to any of her friends for help. Her savings we're down to $17,000 plus the cash she carried in that money clip. Lily took a deep breath and started climbing up the majestic stairway towards the casino.

* * * * *

Brad Summers was feeling very pleased with himself as he surveyed his casino kingdom that Monday night. He had dressed as a gentleman high roller of the Old West, had actually had the entire ensemble made to order from a cast picture of his favorite boyhood television series, the Wild Wild West. In a few minutes, he would open the casino doors and his triumphant evening would begin.

Brad was glad that the casino was up on the second floor-- sequestered away from the rest of the festivities and far away from that pompous British jerk Mark. Brad had met Mark on Saturday night, at a dinner party Patricia had hosted to welcome their master of ceremonies. Mark had been faultlessly polite, but Brad still had the feeling Mark found him and other committee members amusing. Of course, all the women were swooning, charmed by his accent and tall, athletic frame. Brad realized he was likely reading way too much into it. He admitted to himself that at 5' 6" he usually did have a negative opinion towards tall men. They just seemed to all act unjustifiably smug as if their height also conferred some overall superiority.

Brad did not however have the same insecurities towards tall women, and he had spotted a lovely statuesque redhead in a gorgeous green

178

silk gown earlier. He sent up a little prayer to the dating gods that she might visit his casino sometime that evening.

As Brad made his way over to open the doors, he nodded a greeting to a few of the men Bev and her friend Linda had arranged to act as casino security for the evening. He was grateful that Bev had come to his rescue. Eric, another pompous (and tall) jerk had seemed almost pleased to inform Brad that the casino would have to be canceled if security could not be found. The group of guys, all in their 60s mostly from up north, seemed fine--a few seemed a bit rough around the edges but no sense biting a gift horse in the mouth. He had told Bev that the entire rental of tables, roulette wheels, etc. was prepaid and non-refundable. What he hadn't told her was that he had made a second bad decision--it was all on his personal credit card. Well it was a huge amount of travel points and he really wanted to spend Christmas in Saint Lucia again. Of course, Eric had given him a hard time about it before he grudgingly wrote out a check from the VFD fund. Brad never did tell him about the points.

* * * * *

Marisol Martinez had been up since dawn, accepting food deliveries for the Conference Center kitchen. She and her kitchen staff had been working for months to plan, order, cook and freeze the massive amount of food necessary to feed all the attendees. Hors d'oeurves would be consumed throughout the event, a dessert table after midnight, and a massive breakfast buffet would be offered at the end. But Marisol was confused. The flyers that Miguel had brought home advertised the event as a 12-hour marathon starting at 7:00 PM, and finishing at 7:00 AM, in time for the attendees to head to the voting polls in a triumphant parade of Republican consensus. But her kitchen staff was informed by Bev that they would actually be employed for a full 24 hours. The hardworking troop didn't mind. Bev had promised the staff a huge bonus and with Christmas fast approaching, this extra money would be a godsend. They were too excited about their windfall to question why their services were needed for such an extended period. These Leisure Falls residents were always making demands of the staff that seemed to make little sense, so this didn't seem all that unusual.

But Marisol had a mental list in her head of a whole string of things regarding this event that didn't make sense. If it weren't for the fact that her dear little Miguel seemed to be involved, she wouldn't have cared. But Miguel, with his impish grin and mischievous ways, was her heart's love and was quite taken with his new group of friends, especially Matt. Marisol admitted that Miguel had stayed clear of troubles these past months. Matt was clearly a good influence on Miguel and her son regarded this big shaggy man from Wisconsin as a favorite uncle. And both Marisol and Jose had been thrilled to learn that Bev's friend from Chicago had found a summer computer camp for Miguel which had even included a full scholarship. Marisol and Jose often looked at Miguel in amazement. How did that son of theirs have these giant talents? They didn't ever want to stand in his way, but Miguel's involvement in this event made them both uneasy. Jose had calmed Marisol's worries by promising to do a bit of checking around.

* * * * *

Eric and his wife Julie walked slowly down the red carpet, smiling pleasantly but not with the over-the-top giddiness demonstrated by most of the attendees. As one of the wealthiest couples in Leisure Falls, they always behaved with decorum and dignity. Eric, like his fellow committee member Brad, had chosen to dress as a High Roller but there the comparison ended. Eric's suit was of the highest quality with an attention to detail that real money provides. His tie clasp and belt buckle were sterling silver and his hat a made to order Stetson.

Eric certainly looked like a man who had enjoyed a highly successful and lucrative career. As the CEO of Florida's top accounting firm, he and Julie had attended many Republican political fundraisers and had spent more than one evening with Tom Driscoll and his wife. As they neared the entrance, Eric gave his wife an appreciative glance. She was dazzling tonight. Her gown was somewhat more modest in style than many of those worn by the other women. Some of them seemed to be vying for who could show the most cleavage. Julie wore a $10,000 silk Oscar De la Renta ballgown, black with floral and butterfly applique. While the front had a high neckline, the back was open. Elegant, understated, but obviously very expensive. Julie looked like someone who had danced with the President.

As they reached the front door, Mark greeted them with a bow and reminded them to leave all cell phones and watches at the coat check. While Julie complied, Eric, whose phone was stowed in his vest pocket, remarked that he had left it home. "Smart chap," Mark remarked. "Tonight is for celebrating and taking a break from the outside world. I daresay you Yanks will be glued to your mobiles tomorrow."

Eric gave him a perfunctory smile and guided Julie into the Conference Center. He had no qualms over keeping his cell. Eric had not become a CEO by following petty regulations.

* * * * *

Ruthie, likely the youngest attendee of the Victory for Driscoll event, was enjoying a chat with her mom's committee friend Patricia at one of the event's many lounges. She could see why her mom enjoyed Patricia's company. As they sipped on icy gimlets, Patricia was describing her summer spent in upstate New York and entertaining Ruthie with a hilarious story involving a kayak and a Great Dane.

"Ruthie dear, you and your mom should come visit me next summer. There is a darling guesthouse you could stay in."

Ruthie smiled and replied that she was sure they would love that. However, Ruthie knew it was doubtful that Patricia's invitation would still be extended after tomorrow.

Ruthie spied her mom across the room. Her mom looked fabulous. The classy teal blue cocktail dress fit perfectly and Bev's makeup, which Ruthie had applied, made her look years younger. Ruthie could see a glimpse of the Bev who had traveled the globe as a journalist but who had rarely missed one of her kid's tennis matches or piano recitals. Ruthie recognized her mom's expression, one of calm determination and realized it had been many years since she had seen that look of steely resolve. No matter how the event ended, or even the election, this project had been good for her mom. Ruthie waved to her mom. Bev, in return, gave her daughter a smile that was a perfect blend of maternal love, high spirits and confident purpose.

Chapter 29 – Operation Lifesaver – Part 2

Paul directed the movers to hang the final painting on the wall. Spotlights highlighted the Everglades National Park landscape - a sunrise with yellowlegs and blue heron wading in the wetlands. This was a perfect addition to the gallery and any Florida home. It would go to the winner of the of the drawing just before midnight. He stepped to the other side of the room to get the long view – yes, it was perfect.

Gwen was unwrapping the bird sculptures that would be displayed on pedestals in the center of the gallery space. She carefully arranged the pieces varying the heights and styles. She looked at Paul and caught his eye. They were ready. Paul looked at his watch, it was 10:15. He turned on the soft jazz music. Tables with champagne, wine and beer were prepared. Servers with trays of coconut shrimp, sweet and sour meatball appetizers and canapes would arrive as the doors to the gallery opened. In fifteen minutes, the attendees would stream out of the Rachael Stone concert and they would be underway.

. . . .

Meanwhile, David was making his rounds in the casino room with Joey. The other guys on the security team had attended the concert since they were big country music fans, but David was expecting them to arrive at any minute. So far, the crowd seemed to be enjoying themselves.

A small crowd had formed to wait for the casino room doors to open. This was a highlight of the fundraiser event for some of them. At 10:00 pm sharp, Brad had opened the doors and welcomed them in to play slots, blackjack, craps and roulette. Dealers fanned the cards on the tables and smiled at the guests to make them feel comfortable. At the last minute, Brad had convinced Bev to add a couple of poker tables in the back of the room. This was not a bad idea at all since it involved people spending lots of time – sometimes hours – which was right in line with the whole idea for the night. Thirty minutes after getting started the vibe in the room was energetic and the noise level was rising. Folks were ready to have a good time.

"So, this is a nice party David," Joey said as he exchanged his empty Bud Light for a fresh one. "Is there anything else you want me to be doing as, you know, security?"

"Let's just keep to our schedule of making the rounds. From what I can see, the crowd is starting to build, but it all looks good so far. Oh, here come the other guys now," David said. He raised his hand to acknowledge Bobby and Mike who had just entered across the room. They made their way through the crowd.

"That Rachel Stone was a great act- she brought the house down at the end with God Bless the USA. Personally, I think she did it better than Lee Greenwood ever did," said Bobby.

"Salute!" Joey clinked his beer against the others as they all raised a toast. "To a successful fundraiser – and to us for knowing how to enjoy the good life even after all these years."

Mike said. "I will say, these people all look like no trouble at all, but you never know."

"I am going to head over to check in with Linda." said David. "I'll be back in about an hour. Text me if something comes up." David headed out the door and down the long hallway. Chandeliers overhead twinkled setting the ambiance of a party. Bars on each side of the hallway were crowded as people joined friends and really started to enjoy themselves.

.   .   .   .

Linda and Bev looked down at the monitors. Matt had set up additional security cameras so they could see the exact spots they wanted to be able to observe throughout the night. One screen showed the casino, where Linda saw the security team in action. She saw JJ already had a spot at the bar sitting next to a woman dressed up as the woman from the James Bond movie Casino Royale. Even if his attention was on her, Linda knew he also kept an eye on everything going on around him.

Another camera showed the art gallery where Paul and Gwen were talking and gesturing to explain the art to the guests. Everyone had smiles on their faces as they wandered through the gallery. Linda would have to check to see how many raffle tickets had been sold. Waiters were circulating with trays of drinks – looked like all was on track so far.

Matt pointed at the third monitor. "This is what I was telling you about. It seems to be working fine, but then it cuts out. So far it has done this twice and when I went down to check it out there seemed to be nothing wrong. It was working fine."

Bev looked up at Matt to see what point he was trying to make.

"The paranoid side of me thought someone might be interfering with that camera. It is the one that shows hallway leading to the back exit. The kitchen is off to the left and then straight ahead is the exit to the parking lot out back where we all parked our cars. None of the other guests parked there since they came in through the front entrance." Matt crossed his arms and pursed his lips as he methodically thought through the possible explanations. "I don't know, it could be nothing. It is my job to be suspicious of anything that looks awry."

"And we appreciate you doing exactly that" Linda said. "Keep your eyes on that camera. It will be important to us as we leave at the end of the fundraiser. We will need to head right out that door just as breakfast is served and before anyone else leaves."

"Yes, the moment anyone is leaving they will know the truth and we want to be on the road before that happens." Bev said.

"A few minutes ago, I checked the early returns of the election. So far it looks like turnout is very strong in the states where polls already closed. They have called New York and New Jersey for Butler and North Carolina for Driscoll. Most of it is still too early to call, but they are thinking that high turnout will be good for Governor Butler, "Linda said. "Florida is still way too early to call."

Just then David arrived, and they decided to head over to the gallery to check in with Paul and Gwen. Bev decided to find Susan and see how the oxygen bars were working. She wanted to try them out herself, but she also wanted to see how Susan was doing. As she rounded the corner to head back down the main concourse to the front door, she stopped in her tracks to take it all in. People were laughing and dancing. The mood was exciting – like a party just getting started. The voice of Frank Sinatra was belting it out as Bev walked down the stairs and the lyrics fit the mood to a tee...

I've got the world on a string
I'm sitting on the rainbow
I've got that string around my finger
Oh, what a world, and what a life, I'm in love

It was taking Bev quite a while to make her way across the cavernous first floor to check on Susan and the oxygen bar. The stairway and first floor concourse were packed with excited partygoers and Bev was constantly greeted with cries of congratulations over the event and compliments for her gorgeous cocktail dress. She must have chatted with over 40 people in the time it took her to navigate from Matt's surveillance room to the cordoned off area that had been designated as the Vitality Oxy bar.

As Bev neared, she could see what looked like a large cocktail bar arranged in a square, with 20 padded seats along each side of the square. In the center was a huge pyramid of flasks containing both clear and colorful liquids, similar to any cocktail bar with its collection of spirits and liqueurs but there was no alcohol served here - these flasks contained both plain and flavored liquid oxygen and the seven women behind the bar tops were not bartenders but retired nurses. Bev watched as a Leisure Falls couple sat down in the comfortable lounge chairs and were handed menus describing the benefits to be had from a 20-minute oxygen experience, as well as a list of flavored oxygens. Bev overheard the bartender explaining that a 20-minute oxygen shot would provide an energy boost and increased alertness. The couple were then provided with their plastic hoses and the canula that was placed at the entrance of their nostrils. Soon a deep amber flask (cranberry flavor) was attached to the woman's hose and a sea green flask (spearmint) to her husband's. Each of them also received a stack of casino chips, an incentive to encourage ample use of the oxygen bar throughout the long event. The couple seemed to become more energized and Bev promised herself she would make time to try out a few of the flavors before long.

She thought it was ironic that upstairs was a room with the opposite purpose - a dim room filled with Barcaloungers and noise cancelling headphones, allowing patrons to grab a cat nap. Although polar opposites in their approach, both rooms served the same overall goal: keep everyone in the Conference Center until breakfast.

Bell finally spotted the top of Susan's curly blonde head and called out with a cheerful greeting. But Susan raised her head and gave Bev a frown that was almost hostile. Susan gestured that Bev should meet her down the hall. She was obviously upset.

"What the hell is going on here," Susan began "I think you and Linda haven't told me the whole story. I get here this afternoon and I see there's twice as many oxygen cannisters as what I had ordered. Then I see the email requesting my team to stay all day Tuesday. You tell me everything now, everything - or I'm heading home and I'm taking my team with me".

Susan was livid. Her face was flushed, and her fists clenched. Susan was a straight shooter; she didn't play games and she expected her friends to be honest in return. She had put in 35 years as a nurse in Houston, some of those years in the ER and the rest in the operating room. Retired now, she spent much of her time golfing, which is where Bev had met her. Susan's husband Bruce was an avid bird watcher and Bev had joined them for a few forays into the Everglades with The Peepers, the Leisure Falls bird watching club. On the golf course or with The Peepers, Susan was a lot of fun. She had a bawdy sense of humor that never quite crossed the line but flirted with it. Bev had never seen this side of her and was really regretting keeping her out of the loop. This was a miscalculation on her part.

Although Bev was rattled at the extent of Susan's anger, she managed to spell out the whole plan. Beth could see Susan's ire abating and she breathed a sigh of relief. Bev needed Susan's cooperation as the oxygen bar might end up being an integral part in keeping the attendees engaged and energized throughout the event.

"You know, I smelled a rat back when you joined the fundraiser committee. I shoulda known you wouldn't suddenly support that dog Driscoll, not after all the hours we spent trashing him. But I'm really hurt you didn't trust me enough to include me in your plan. "

Bev went on to explain to Susan that she had kept her from the full story for Susan's own benefit, so that she wouldn't have to answer to any accusations later that week. It was possible that things could get very ugly and everyone's role in the event would be scrutinized. Bev could see that Susan was beginning to understand the scope of the plan- both the hoped-for results and the likely consequences for participating.

"Well Bev, I guess I get it and although I'm still a bit pissed, I do appreciate why you kept me out of the loop. You've always been a good friend and you thought you needed to protect me, but Bev I'm from Texas and we never back down from a fight. I'm in the loop now. I despise that man, he's not worth spit. I'm gonna take part in this, even knowing I'll have a few nasty conversations later this week. Bruce would agree, so he's in too.

So now that I am an official member of.... what did you call it... Operation Lifesaver? - I think you could really use my help. We've had a few dozen folks come up and use the oxygen but you're gonna need way more customers if these folks are to make it through this entire event. How about if I send Bruce and a few of my gals out to drum up some business? They can hand out menus and a few chips with the promise of more if they get hooked up to some O's."

"Susan, that's brilliant. Thank you from the bottom of my heart."

Bev left the oxygen bar, feeling grateful for the help but a bit ashamed that she had underestimated her friend. She headed back to the control center to fill Linda in.

* * * * *

Enzo "The Voice" settled into a seat at the casino bar, ordered a vodka tonic and perused the bar menu. He had heard that the casino had the best food at the event: meatballs, bruschetta, scampi and little veal parmesan sliders - all his favorites and all things he had given up in order to lose 50 pounds. He loosened up the bottom button on his tuxedo vest in anticipation of the mini feast he had just ordered. Enzo had been blessed at birth in three ways: a huge appetite, especially for the food his Ma made back home in Hoboken, a heart of gold with a warm gregarious personality and the voice of an angel. Only 24, Lorenzo, or for short, Enzo had become an overnight sensation on *America's Great Singers*, capturing both the audience's and the judge's admiration with his silken renditions of hits from Frank Sinatra, Dean Martin and Tony Bennett. His manager, Enzo's Uncle Vinny, had nagged and harangued Enzo to lose weight, finally convincing him to get serious about sticking to a low carb diet and exercise regimen. Now after 14 months of torture, Enzo looked great. He would never be skinny, but Uncle Vinny was satisfied, and his bookings were going through the roof. Vinny had stayed back in New Jersey for this gig, so Enzo felt safe in a little indulgence. After all, he was booked for a 90-minute slot in the early morning hours and he would need some extra energy. Maybe he would even have time for some blackjack.

By the time the server began spreading out an embarrassing amount of small plates onto the bar top, Enzo was chatting with a couple of older guys. He soon learned that Joey and Mike were part of a security team that would ensure that no trouble occurred within the casino. Even though Joey and Mike were from Chicago, they reminded him of his uncles back home. Joey was medium height and lean with a shock of black curly hair while Mike was shorter, stocky and almost bald.

Enzo made friends easily and before long, plates were being shared. Joey insisted that Enzo had to sample the calamari and soon even more dishes were delivered to the bar: crispy fried squid with a spicy arrabbiata sauce, a steaming bowl of garlicky muscles and a platter of baked clams. Enzo laughed uproariously when Mike divulged that the security team, all aging members of a long defunct softball team, were being paid with drinks and food. Mike had insisted on an all Italian menu and had worked with the kitchen staff several weeks ago to ensure that the casino was indeed supplied with the best food of the event. The three soon declared themselves paisanos and Joey took Enzo to introduce him to the rest of the guys.

They found JJ and Bobby at a nearby blackjack table. Both men had enormous stacks of $100 chips in front of them and both were sipping on tumblers of Scotch. Enzo had a great time talking to Bobby, tall and elegantly dressed, who recognized Enzo and was a big fan.

"Joey, do you live in a cave up there in Chicago? How can you not know about Enzo the Voice? This guy's got pipes that are as smooth as this 20-year old Scotch."

"Don't jump all over me Bobby. I don't watch TV. I just thought he was a nice kid."

Bobby turned to Enzo "If you have time tomorrow, come on down to my place with the guys. Play some golf. I got a real nice set up a few hours south of here, real classy. Hey JJ, you recognize this kid, right?"

JJ was sitting next to Bobby but was not paying any attention. He only had eyes for the gorgeous redhead on his other side. JJ had spent the last hour chatting up Lily Barton and not getting very far. All he knew was that she lived at Leisure Falls, had done well with a fancy-dress shop and was wearing a silk gown that showed off a very fine figure. He was just about to ask for her number when he heard raised voices over by the craps table.

Joey, Mike and Bobby rushed over to see what the commotion was all about. They found Eric arguing with a man almost twice his size wearing worn jeans that were not altogether clean and a blue cotton work shirt. The man's burly 6-foot frame towered over Eric as he bent down to point an angry finger in Eric's face. The man, identified as Larry by the name embroidered on his shirt pocket, was clearly drunk and clearly infuriated with Eric, who to his credit, did not back down. Joey slid between the men while Mike and Bobby stationed themselves on either side, silently flanking the huge cowboy.

"Now what's going on here?" Joey looked relaxed and sounded reasonable.

"This little pissant won't turn on the TVs so I can see how the football turned out. I had money riding on that game." The man gestured towards all the TV monitors which were black. "He says they aren't hooked up, but I know that can't be true. I was just here for a party last week and they worked fine then."

Before Joey could work on diffusing the situation, Eric snarled back, "If you cared so much about the stupid game, you big asshole, you should have stayed back in your trailer home drinking your warm Budweiser. How'd you get in here anyway? I don't think you even live in Leisure Falls. You look like a loser to me."

Joey was stunned that Eric would have the balls to engage this guy who must have weighed 70 pounds more and was 15 years younger. You almost had to admire the man. But Eric had had his lifetime fill of men who were bullies because they were both stupid and big. He took one step closer and slowly, deliberately gave Larry his middle finger. This was all it took for chaos to erupt. It turned out that Larry had a couple of buddies with him, all big, all drunk and all under 60. JJ tossed back the last of his Scotch and lept into the fray and Enzo, without even being asked, also joined in to help his new buddies. A few uncoordinated punches were thrown. A couple of bloody nose noses ruined some very expensive cowboy shirts. In the end, Bev and Linda's security team prevailed, just as they had all those years ago.

When David burst in, wild eyed with panic, having seen the fracas from the security monitors, the fellas from Chicago were all grinning and slapping each other on the backs. Enzo, holding some ice up to a split lip, was laughing with Eric, of all people, who looked as if his Wild Wild West fantasy dreams had just come true.

Miraculously none of the rented gaming tables had been damaged and the gamblers were all slowly returning to their games. Some of them thought that the fight had been staged as entertainment depicting a real Old West dustup. Larry and his posse were sobering up, looking sheepish and embarrassed, partly because of their boorish behavior but mostly due to the fact that they had just gotten whooped by a bunch of oldsters with bad knees.

For the past 20 minutes all eyes had been on the fight. No one had noticed that an attractive woman of a certain age in a stunning emerald gown had quietly gathered all the chips at the blackjack table and slipped out of the casino.

Linda reached for a second coconut shrimp. They were crunchy on the outside and perfectly tender on the inside. A little dip in the spicy mango sauce and they were irresistible. Even with all she had on her mind, Linda took a deep breath and relished the tasty treat. Yes, this was work in a sense, but it was also the party they had planned for almost a year. It was going well so far, and she was going to enjoy herself for a few minutes.

Paul was just finishing up selling raffle tickets to a group of four couples. Everyone wanted the large Everglades painting so each couple bought 10 tickets. Paul smiled and told them each to be sure to come back for the grand drawing at midnight. He came over to where David and Linda were standing.

"We are selling a lot of these raffle tickets. There is a lot of interest, so I think we included a good selection for this group. I think I will even have some follow-on business out of this event," Paul said.

"Well, they are certainly having a good time tonight, we will see how happy they are in the morning," Linda said.

David snagged a meatball as a tray went by. "I don't see Gwen, is she around somewhere?"

"She went downstairs to try out the oxygen bar. As the night wears on she is determined to stay awake, so she doesn't miss anything."

"Usually Gwen is very cool and reserved at our art events. Very Audrey Hepburn in Breakfast at Tiffany's. But she is unbelievably excited about this" said Paul. He adjusted his dark rimmed glasses and straightened his tie. "I think it is also the fact that we live in Florida ourselves now, so we are contributing to the election outcome. In the past, Florida has been at the heart of controversy in these elections – chads and all that. This time, we want to right a wrong that has been done. This has been a long time in coming and we are both committed to playing our role."

"Paul, you and Gwen are certainly contributing your share and more," Linda said. "I can't tell you how much we appreciate your efforts to help us with our plan."

They wandered through the gallery looking at the art, but also listening to the guests to get a sense of the mood. A group of several women gathered around a painting of a landscape scene. Sun sparkled off the blue water of a lagoon surrounded by grasses and wildflowers. David and Linda stood behind the group to observe and listen while making it look as though they were also focused on the painting.

"To me, the colors and textures in this one would be just perfect for our foyer, "said a tall woman wearing a Moroccan-style kaftan in turquoise with gold floral brocade.

"This gallery exhibit has so many interesting pieces, I just want to make sure I bring one home so I can remember this night. I am having the time of my life," said one of the other women.

A blond wearing white jewelry to offset her tan and hot pink gown drained her champagne glass and added, "I never thought I would be so interested in art, but I love way he tells the story behind each piece and the artist who painted it."

The group moved on to examine the next painting and erupted in laughter as one of them gestured to the painting, imitating how Paul would explain the piece and the artist.

"Well, they certainly are having a good time," Linda said. "I see Edna from the fundraiser committee over there. I think I will go over and say hello."

"According to my watch, it is 12:30 Operation Lifesaver time so we are halfway through the night" David said as he glanced down and quickly hid his watch. "It's time for me to head back to the casino, I will catch up with you later."

Linda waved at Edna who was talking with Gwen. As she moved past all the guests crowded around the bird sculptures, Linda noticed Edna was pointing up at the ceiling. "Hi Edna, it is so nice to see you again."

"Linda, I am so glad you are here. The whole evening has been fabulous so far." Edna turned to smile at Linda and her eyes sparkled with enjoyment. "I think everyone is picking up energy as the night goes on. Gwen was just telling me about how they design these gallery exhibits and the work that goes into displaying the pieces so that they are shown in the best way."

"Yes, Edna seems to have a good eye for the complications involved. It all looks so perfect when we are ready, but the steps to getting there are tedious, but so important to achieve the overall effect we want." Gwen was stunning in a long black gown with a v neckline, low back and ruching across the body that created a slimming effect.

"You both look fabulous this evening," Linda said.

"Well, thank-you. It is no easy job to keep it all together for a long night like this. We will do our best." Edna tilted her head to one side and thought for a moment. "If the clock says 1:00 am, then I suppose we are heading into the final 12 hours. It is starting to look like we might pull this off! I'm going to the casino for a few hands of blackjack!" She winked at a stunned Linda and waved as she headed out the door.

"Did she just say what I think she said?" Gwen asked.

"I think she did, she knows the clocks in the convention center are not showing the correct time and she seems to know that there is something more going on here tonight than just a good party." Linda's mind was racing as she tried to think of the implications of what Edna had just said.

"Well, she seems to be on-board with the idea," said Gwen. "At least it seems as though she is just happily waiting to see how it all turns out – like it is part of the fun."

"Yes, did you see that she winked at me?" Linda asked. "She was letting me know that she knows something. I need to find Bev right away and tell her what just happened. Keep up the good work here – we will catch up with you later as planned." Linda gave Gwen a quick hug and hurried out in search of Bev.

.   .   .   .   .

Mark was at the bar on the main floor with the microphone. As he looked up and down the concourse, he saw people with drinks sitting in groups relaxing. They looked a little too relaxed – this is where he came in.

"Thank-you so much for being with us this evening and supporting the cause." Mark boomed into the microphone. As he clinked his glass of water with a spoon, the conversations gradually subsided into low murmurs while people turned to give Mark their attention.

"As you all know, we are here for a fundraiser, so hear is where the _fun_ in fundraiser comes in. I know this crowd is a little competitive on the golf courses – but tonight, you are going to get your chance to exercise your muscle memory for a couple of fun competitions. The most exciting news on this is that there will be prizes for the winners! At breakfast, I will announce the names of 6 lucky couples who will each win a deluxe around the world cruise on Viking!".

At the mention of these prizes a roar went up from the crowd and enthusiastic whistling and applause encouraged Mark to keep going.

"First, you should know that I will be the judge of all contests and will have both the first and final word on all winners." Mark gave a wide sweep of his arm to show how all-powerful he would be, and smiled broadly, eliciting groans from some and cheering from others.

"We will have a great time and those of you who play your cards right, so to speak, will also have bragging rights until the next fundraiser. Is everyone ready to start?"

Groups pulled their chairs closer to be near the action. Music started playing and Mark brought out a big gong that he demonstrated by hitting once.

"See, this is all about memory and singing. We will start by playing a song you likely remember very well from your youth. Let's hear you sing along with this one." The opening of *Laughter in the Rain* by Neil Sedaka started, and everyone sang along for a couple of lines until the music abruptly stopped.

> Strolling along country roads with my baby
> It starts to rain, it begins to pour
> Without an umbrella we're soaked to the skin
> I feel a shiver run up my spine

"Now, we want whoever I point at to sing the next lines in the song. Which in this case is..." Mark put his hand up to cup his ear and waited for the crowd to sing . . .

> Oh, I hear laughter in the rain,
> Walking hand in hand with the one I love
> Oh, how I love the rainy days and the happy way I feel inside

"Excellent, Very good. Ok, now you see how it will go. Let's get started - Play the first song!". The unmistaken beat of the Rolling Stones came on.

> I can't get no satisfaction, I can't get no satisfaction
> 'Cause I try and I try and I try and I try
> I can't get no, I can't get no

Linda watched as the groups began to engage and participate in the game. Just as she remembered from the Viking cruise, Mark had them all in the palm of his hand. Some of the people really got into it and insisted on coming up to sing into the microphone. Others danced and sang their lines – bringing the crowd to their feet in appreciation.

Assured that Mark had things well in hand, Linda headed back to the control center to meet with Bev. Operation Lifesaver time was now at 1:30 am meaning real EST was now almost 8 hours ahead. As she approached, Linda saw everyone gathered around the monitors. Bev was nervously walking around the back of the group peering in to get a glimpse.

"What is the latest?" Linda asked"

"Well, in terms of Operation Lifesaver, everything is going according to plan and on schedule," said Matt. "I have checked the cameras and they are all operating, the clocks are all working and showing the Operation Lifesaver time." He clicked through a series of screens to check cameras.

"In terms of the election, everything is still up in the air," said Bev. Right now, Driscoll has a lead of 16,000 votes in Florida, but they have not yet finished counting the votes in Broward and Sumter counties."

"What do we know about the electoral map?" Linda asked.

Matt scanned the room before clicking on the latest version of the electoral map which showed Democrats currently with 232 and Republican with 204 electoral votes. Several states including Texas, Arizona, Minnesota, Michigan and Pennsylvania - along with Florida still were not yet decided.

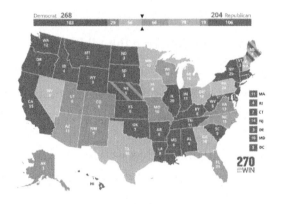

"We need Florida and one other state," said David. "Even Arizona with only 11 electoral votes would put us over the top."

"I'm keeping my fingers crossed," said Linda. "Just a few more hours and the fundraiser will be over. How is everything going in the casino room?"

"It's going great, Enzo Valentino came by and met the guys. They really hit it off and are enjoying themselves at the bar, while keeping an eye on everything."

"Sounds perfect," said Bev. "Enzo is due for his performance in about 1 hour from now. I can't wait to hear him sing. The crowd will love it!"

They all started to split up to rejoin the party.

---

[3] https://www.270towin.com/

"I just had a shocking moment with Edna and Gwen over by the art gallery." Linda pulled Bev to the side and filled her in on what had happened.

"Well, I'm not surprised, Edna has been in on the committee meetings, she has met with you a couple of times, she knows my politics and what LF means to the overall outcome of the election in Florida. Even though we haven't brought her in on everything, I believe she could figure it out." Bev reviewed the facts out loud.

"Do you think we need to talk with her and bring her in to the rest of the plan for Operation Lifesaver?" Linda asked.

"No. No, the more I think about it, the more it seems that she is telling us all we need to know. She will be behind us 100% and not just for the fundraiser, but also for Operation Lifesaver. I think we are safe, leaving it just as it is. Let's go back and see how Mark is doing with the singing competition."

Bev and Linda walked back to the concourse together. Matt had also briefly stepped from the control center to get an Italian beef sandwich for his dinner. Nobody noticed Miguel on the camera by the back door. He had a gigantic plate of appetizers in each hand and was headed out the door.

Bev peered into the napping room. She was able to discern through the dim lighting that almost all the 250 Barcaloungers were filled. It had been a great idea of Ruthie's to provide the noise cancelling headphones as more than a few nappers were quite loud, snores and snorts erupting in a cacophony of sleeping noises. The town hall style rally would begin soon, followed by the event headliner Enzo The Voice and then breakfast along with the grand prize raffle. So far, so good. She quietly shut the door and headed downstairs to the small ballroom where the rally was to begin.

When Bev entered the small ballroom, she found Patricia chatting with Jesse Faulkner and his TV partner Amy Dean. Both were well-known commentaries for Fox News and, like most employees of Fox, big Driscoll supporters. Patricia, with her many Washington DC connections, had managed to convince Fox News that the Victory for Driscoll event was newsworthy and that an election eve rally for Driscoll would be a great feature for Faulkner's Sunday morning show, Jawing with Jesse.

Patricia had persuaded the Fox News executives that not only were the residents of Leisure Falls an important Republican voting bloc but that they, as a community, represented a large segment of Fox viewers in Florida.

When Patricia had suggested at the April committee meeting, that the fundraiser should include a televised rally, everyone on the committee had been wildly enthusiastic, everyone except Bev. The committee had been thrilled at the notion that Leisure Falls would be featured on a national television program and they were all fans of Jesse Faulkner. Bev had smiled and feigned great interest but inside she had been dying. She knew that Patricia would be personally mortified to have been an unknowing pawn in this ruse. Bev and Linda had speculated that Leisure Falls would likely cover up the fact that they had been fooled into missing the voting. They would be too embarrassed to admit that they had been gambling, dancing and drinking away the hours when the polls were open, and the nation was voting for the next President of the United States.

As the lighting and sound technicians finished readying for taping, guests poured into the room and found places to sit. Ushers handed out small American flags and large colorful buttons that showed the Victory for Driscoll emblem. The mood was festive bordering on raucous. The lights dimmed and out strode Jesse and Amy, smiling broadly and waving to the crowd who were now on their feet, waving their flags and cheering. This rally would definitely energize the crowd. Eventually the noise level abated and Jesse, slim and handsome, wearing a navy suit with a scarlet tie, started addressing the room.

"What a happy day this is, and Fox News is thrilled to celebrate with the great folks of Leisure Falls. I'm Jesse Faulkner, here with the lovely Amy Dean. We want our viewers to get to know this fantastic community of Driscoll supporters. We want to hear your stories and we definitely want to make some noise."

Predictably the crowd responded with more cheers and vigorous flag waving. A chant began towards the back of the room- Leisure Falls for Driscoll, Leisure Falls for Driscoll- and soon everyone joined in. Bev smiled and gave thanks that no one in this rowdy crowd would want to go home early.

It took even longer for the crowd to quiet enough for Jesse to start talking again. He had just begun to introduce the first scheduled speaker, Fred Williams, CEO of Leisure Falls, when a figure burst onto the stage. Bev couldn't see who it was from her spot in the back of the ballroom. All she could make out was that it was a tall man in a black tux, wildly upset, arms flailing. Bev gasped when she realized it was Eric. Calm, arrogant, unflappable Eric who rarely showed any emotion stronger than cool disdain. Bev thought at first that he was in the midst of a major coronary. Amy Dean rushed over, but Eric shoved her aside causing her to trip on the TV cables and fall to her knees. Eric stumbled over to Jesse, who stood with his mouth wide open in astonishment. Jesse seemed paralyzed into total inaction and Eric easily grabbed the microphone from him.

"We've been duped. This is a trick people. The time on the clocks......."

A man dressed in khakis and a blue polo dashed across the stage and wrested the microphone from Eric before he could finish his warning. Bev couldn't believe her eyes. The man, now wrestling with Eric to gain control over the mike, appeared to be Nelson Grimes, the security chief for Leisure Falls. Grimes was assumed to be sailing down the Volga River in Russia, participating in a security consortium. In fact, just a few days ago, he had sent an email to the security office boasting of how impressed the other participants were with the system he had set up in Florida.

Bev rubbed her eyes. Was this a mirage? What was Grimes doing back at Leisure Falls and what was he doing up on the stage grappling with Eric? Eric's face was getting even redder. Grimes shorter but stockier was slowly overpowering him. Jesse, finally regaining his wits, was beckoning to the film crew to stop taping and come help.

The crowd was stunned. They were at a loss to how to react. Many of them knew Eric; he was active in various committees. With the film crew jumping in, Eric was subdued and forced off the stage, albeit still struggling. Bev could see that Grimes had his hand placed firmly across Eric's mouth, preventing him from finishing whatever message he so desperately had wanted to impart. Amy Dean was helped to her feet and walked rather gingerly back to center stage. Jesse addressed the room with his retrieved microphone.

"Well folks everything's OK. The gentleman was a bit disoriented but is fine now. I heard the drinks up at the casino are all doubles"

The crowd chuckled nervously. The ones that knew Eric personally understood that he would never overindulge, especially in public. But what other explanation could there be?

Before anyone could dwell on it for too long, Jesse nodded to a few members of the audience, a group that had been deliberately coached before-hand to ratchet up the enthusiasm if needed. Soon cries of "Leisure Falls for Driscoll" once again reverberated. At this point, Bev slipped out of the ballroom and ran straight into the very person she needed to talk to - Matt.

"Whoa sis, everything's OK.... I think. The problem is contained and by the problem I mean Eric. He kept his phone and somehow has a program on it that overrides the Internet dead zone that I had installed. He now knows what we're up to or at least that voting is occurring across the country and our fundraiser event is keeping the Leisure Falls population away from the polls."

Bev wasn't too surprised that Eric had kept his phone. Eric had always felt that he was too important to follow any rules or restrictions imposed on the ordinary resident. But it was worrisome that Matt's software program was not impervious. Matt had successfully reset all the clocks within the Conference Center to run more slowly. At the same time, he had ensured that the entire community of Leisure Falls was an Internet dead zone - no current news would be available. Bev had no idea how Matt had managed this, but its success was key to Operation Lifesaver. And then there was the question of Grimes.

"But Matt, how did Grimes get here and more importantly why is he here?"

"Now that is something I'm working on. He showed up an hour ago. Didn't say much- just gave me his usual slimy sneer and said that thanks to him, everything would work out. I have no idea what he meant. Then I saw on the monitors upstairs the big fiasco on stage. I don't understand what Grimes is up to. What is he even doing here? Does he know our plans? Is he going to help us or hurt us? In four and a half hours the polls will close. We are so close Bev."

"Where is Eric right now? And what about his wife? Won't she be worried?"

"Grimes took Eric out of the building and over to the security office. He texted me that Eric will remain there until the event is over. Geez, I hope Grimes won't do anything stupid. I already thought of Eric's wife. She was over in the main ballroom with her girlfriends. They were playing that music contest Mark is running. I texted Mark- he's going to have her group win some VIP seating at that concert that's coming up, with that Frank Sinatra singer guy. She'll be too busy to worry about the hubby. Mark said that she and her pals were pounding down the cocktails. With any luck, she won't know or care that Eric just made the scene of his life in front of 3000 people."

. . . . . .

Several hours later Marisol and her staff worked frantically to refill the chafing dishes and platters at the breakfast buffet. Most of them had skipped the concert to sneak up to the napping room and catch a few hours of rest and it was a good thing they had. Everyone seemed ravenous and the mounds of pancakes, sausages and bacon seemed to disappear minutes after they had been replenished. The lines for the made-to-order omelets snaked around the room.

Even Miguel was pressed into service and was sent out with carafes of orange juice to fill up glasses. Marisol did not mind at all that Miguel was under foot. She wanted to keep an eye on him- he could get into mischief faster than lightning. The event was nearing an end, successfully it seemed to her if you could go by the copious amounts of food being consumed and the loud happy sounding chatter emanating from the hundreds of roundtables set up in the ballroom. She had never seen so many dressed up people sitting down to breakfast, although she knew it was early evening. Miguel had also figured out how to circumvent the so-called Internet dead zone. He had sworn his mother to secrecy -he didn't want his" Uncle Matt" to be mad.

Marisol carried out yet another huge platter of pastries just in time to hear that fellow from England announce that the grand prize raffle would begin shortly.

"Before I announce the six winners, I want everyone to give Mrs. Marisol Martinez and her staff a round of applause in appreciation for this amazing breakfast. It was so delicious that I didn't even miss the baked beans and roasted tomato that we Brits enjoy."

Marisol could feel the blood rushing to her face as thousands enthusiastically applauded. Marisol was not used to being in the spotlight. She shyly waved, hoping that the extra attention might inspire some of these wealthy attendees to leave a tip - her hardworking ladies certainly deserved it after this marathon.

Mark continued, "Now while you finish your coffee and pastries, I am going to announce the winners of our grand prize. Six lucky winners will choose a companion to join them on a deluxe 2-month Viking ocean excursion around the world. Airfare is included as well as all day excursions. This will indeed be the trip of a lifetime. May I have the lights dim and a drumroll please. The first winner of the Victory for Driscoll grand prize raffle is . . . Marcy Walker! Please join me on the stage Marcy."

215

The crowd applauded wildly, craning their necks to spot the lucky winner. After a few seconds, the spotlights found her. Marisol could see an older woman clad in a tight shiny fuchsia dress jumping up and down. She began making her way up to the stage, pulling behind her a man who Marisol assumed was her husband. He also looked happy but sheepish too and seemed to be limping a bit.

Mark helped Marcy up the steps to the stage, still with limping husband in tow and guided her over to the microphone. An usher presented her with a tremendous bouquet of fresh flowers. Petals flew across the stage as Marcy was still jumping up and down, too excited to stand still.

"Marcy, you certainly seemed thrilled. These flowers are taking quite a beating." Mark chuckled and the crowd joined in, sharing in Marcy's obvious elation.

"Now, is this the lucky chap that will join you on this once in a lifetime cruise?"

"Oh yes. This is my husband Howie. We've always wanted to travel but never could what with raising our boys. This is a dream come true."

A new spray of petals flew as Marcy resumed her jumping.

Marisol watched for a few minutes until she spotted Miguel waving frantically from the kitchen door. She ran over, sure that Miguel had caused some kind of catastrophe in the kitchen. Marisol didn't see a heap of shattered dishes or upset trays of pastries as she had feared. Instead she found Miguel patting the shoulder of Bev who was propped up against the tiled wall with an ice bag on a hugely swollen ankle that was rapidly turning a deep shade of purple. An elderly woman wearing a sort of ropy green dress was propping up her leg on a stack of kitchen towels. Marisol thought her name might be Edna from things Miguel had said. It was obvious that Bev was in a lot of pain. But bit by bit she managed to relate what had happened.

. . . . . .

Bev and Ruthie had been enjoying a well-earned breakfast together. They had filled up plates with bacon and scrambled eggs and found a quiet corner outside the main ballroom to enjoy their feast. Bev had been too nervous and revved up to have eaten much of anything throughout the event. Now that the fund raiser was nearly over and it appeared that they had miraculously kept an entire Conference Center of elderly Republican voters entertained and distracted for 24 hours, she was relaxed enough to feel famished.

They were having fun regaling each other with all the funny and unexpected things that had happened. Ruthie had filled Bev in on the big casino free-for-all. Ruthie had been trying her luck at blackjack when the melee had begun. Ruthie was almost laughing too hard to talk as she told her mom that most of the guests had assumed the fight had been staged as entertainment. Some had even given the troublemakers casino chips as a tip to express their appreciation at what they had thought were choreographed stunts. Ruthie had also spotted a gorgeous looking older woman making off with stacks of stolen ships from the adjacent blackjack table when everyone else had been focused on the fight.

Another fight had almost ensued when it was discovered that the chips were gone. Ruthie had decided not to share her knowledge of the whereabouts of the missing chips. She was intrigued by the mystery woman in green and had admired the daring that it must have taken to abscond with such a fortune in plain sight. Bev and Ruthie pondered what the woman's story was and what she might do with all that money.

Bev in turn had told Ruthie about the close call with Eric and the unexpected appearance of Nelson Grimes. Matt had still not filled her in as to why Grimes had returned to Leisure Falls before his Russian cruise had ended. She assumed that the Eric situation was under control. There was only 45 minutes left until the buffet ended, so whatever disruption he had hoped to cause had not come to pass.

Bev could hear that Mark was announcing that the raffle would be beginning soon. This was her signal to leave through the kitchen, collect her car and pick up Ruthie by the side entrance. She gave Ruthie a quick kiss.

"See you in about 20 minutes. You change clothes now; I'll change at a rest stop later. "

Bev left Ruthie and walked briskly through the ballroom and into the kitchen. She grabbed her purse that she had stowed by the dishwashers and left through the kitchen door, waving up at the monitor where she knew Matt was watching. She mouthed a thank you and blew him a kiss.

As she exited the kitchen, she felt the humid Florida air. It felt good after spending the last 24 hours in the dry chilly air conditioning of the

Conference Center. She ran to the back of the parking lot where she had left her car, all packed and ready to go. And stopped short. Two trucks were blocking her car. They were both burgundy colored with a colorful yellow insignia on the side which read Juanita's Lavanderia. One of the trucks had its hood up and was spewing a large plume of steam. Bev started to panic as she didn't see the drivers around. She had only 30 minutes before the conference doors opened. Bev turned to run back into the kitchen, but her high heel caught on a crack in the asphalt and she went down hard, twisting her ankle painfully as she fell. Bev lay on the warm asphalt, feeling nauseous from both the pain and the shock. She fought to keep down the eggs and bacon she had happily consumed just a little earlier. How stupid she thought. Why didn't I put on some sneakers before I left the kitchen? What an idiot I am.

Bev started crying from the pain, from exhaustion, from frustration. She was not going to make the clean escape that Linda and she had planned and Ruthie would also get dragged into what was going to be an ugly confrontation. But Beth had not counted on a guardian angel, someone who had been watching everything from a distance, someone who had been watching out for her.

"Bev dear, can I be of assistance?"

Edna had appeared out of nowhere. Bev was so stunned to see her that she could only mutely nod. Edna helped Bev get up and supported her enough so that Bev could hobble back to the kitchen. It was good to be off the hard asphalt parking lot, but Bev knew that she was still in big trouble. Her ankle was bad, maybe broken, badly sprained at best. Even if the disabled laundry truck could be moved, Bev would not be able to drive her car.

Edna put together an ice bag for Bev and tried to make her a little more comfortable. Bev began to ask Edna what she had been doing out in the parking lot, but Edna brushed away her questions.

"You don't have time to hear about it Bev. The fundraiser will be ending in 15 minutes. We have to get you out of here so you and Ruthie can join Linda up in Chicago."

Bev could only look at Edna incredulously "Did Matt tell you about the whole plan?"

"No Bev, I just kept my mouth shut and my eyes and ears opened. It really wasn't hard to figure out. I'm not quite as doddering as you might think. I heard enough snippets to put it all together. Your lovely brother just thinks I lent a hand with the programming. I was a bit more involved than that but that's a story for another day. Oh good, here comes Marisol. I bet she can figure out how to get you on your way."

Edna quickly told Marisol about the problem with the disabled laundry truck and Marisol could clearly see the problem with Bev's ankle. She appeared completely unsurprised that Bev was trying to leave the fancy event via her kitchen door instead of through the front entrance as one might expect a committee member to do. Bev wondered just how many people were aware of her and Linda's plans.

Marisol was used to solving any problem that arose in her kitchen, even ones that didn't pertain to food. The broken- down laundry truck could not be started, and Bev couldn't drive anyway. Ruthie could certainly drive but she was waiting by the side entrance and the car was blocked in by the laundry truck. Marisol needed Plan B, and her younger cousin Juanita, owner of the best commercial laundry service in Central Florida, was happy to help. Thanks to Marisol, Juanita's Lavanderia had the exclusive contract for the Leisure Falls Conference Center. Juanita owed Marisol a debt of gratitude. She would personally drive the truck all the way to the Tampa airport and ensure that Bev and her daughter Ruthie were safely aboard the plane.

Bev wondered if she had suffered a concussion out in the parking lot. Everything was happening so fast and nobody thought it at all odd that a 60-year-old woman wearing a lovely teal cocktail dress was being loaded into the back of a laundry truck.

Chapter 33 – Operation Lifesaver – Part 6

They were reaching the big conclusion of the fundraiser. Not only were people on their feet, they were still enjoying themselves. They had to keep everyone engaged for another 3 hours and they had the right guy to do it. Enzo Valentino would perform for 90 minutes and between the Las Vegas, Frank Sinatra style music and his charismatic personality, Linda felt sure they would get to their end goal.

There was a slow drift of the crowd toward the ball room. Some guests had purchased a 10 seat round table surrounding the enormous dance floor. Early arrivers might still be able to get a table, or they would stand up to high-top tables around the edge of the ball room. Many people had tickets to the second and third level seats which accommodated 30,000 fans for other events.

Mark joined Linda and Bev as they headed to the massive ball room for the concert. The casino was still open, so JJ and Bobby stayed to keep an eye on things, while David, Paul and Gwen headed up to the ball room.

Backstage, the band was arriving and getting into place. The speakers softly played warm-up music which would gradually crescendo until a drum roll quieted the crowd for Mark's introduction of Enzo Valentino.

. . . .

In the hallway, a loud and angry voice rose above the crowd excitement. Linda and Mark looked at each other with anxiety. They were hyper-alert to anything happening that would throw Operation Lifesaver off track.

"I'm going to see what is going on out there," Linda said.

"I'll come with you in case you need a hand." Mark followed Linda back through the tables and out the door of the ballroom. They quickly saw the source of the disruption - a confrontation between a large man in a cowboy hat and one of the staff.

"I'm telling you; I need my phone now!" the man shouted.

Linda and Mark hurried over to de-escalate the situation, "Can I be of some assistance here?" Mark asked as he joined the group.

"This gentleman is insisting that he needs his phone to check his medication schedule," the staffer said. "I know we aren't supposed to have anyone with a phone this evening. I don't know what to do."

"I'll tell you what to do, find my phone immediately! This is no game, I need to make sure I am sticking with my medication schedule. A missed dose can land me back in the hospital!" The man looked back and forth at their faces to see if his complaint was going to be addressed.

"Of course, that is a very good reason for us to find your phone for you," Linda reassured the man. "I believe the phones were checked in up front, near the entrance, when everyone arrived. Mark, will you assist this gentleman and make sure he gets exactly what he needs?"

Linda exchanged a meaningful look with Mark, and he understood completely. With Operation Lifesaver operating on a different time schedule, they had checked with medical experts to be sure that the time change would not raise an issue with medication schedules. The whole team had been briefed on this and the contingency plan if a question came up. Was this guy could on the level or was he using this as an excuse to cause trouble? He looked harmless, but Linda knew that it was a risk to ignore him. They were so close to the end; they could not afford to take a chance.

"Allow me to escort you and your lovely wife over to the check-in station and we will get to the bottom of this immediately." Mark made a gallant gesture pointing toward the front of the building and away from where the crowd was gathering for the big performance.

The big man took a deep breath, relaxed and allowed himself to be maneuvered back around the counter. He took his wife's arm and Mark reassuringly put his hand on the man's shoulder and began walking them both away from the crowded ballroom. Linda held her breath for a few seconds until she saw a smile on the wife's face as she replied to a question from Mark. Apparently, the situation had been diffused and Linda gave a quick prayer of thanks for having Mark on the team. She texted Mark that he should encourage the couple to return to the performance if it looked like a non-issue. She had every confidence in Mark and would leave it in his hands.

. . . .

Back in the ballroom the lights were signaling that the show was about to start. The full band was in place and they were starting to play the opening number. The audience was ready and looking forward to a great

225

concert. Most of LV had watched America's Great Singers and had fallen in love with Enzo. From his first audition, he said he wanted his music to be fun and to make people happy. Some performers have the knack of showing real authentic personality and Enzo was clearly this kind of a performer.

"And now, please welcome a familiar face. We all came to know and love him on *America's Great Singers* where he wowed the judges and the fans. Our final performer for the evening, The Voice - Enzo Valentino."

The stage lit up, Enzo came onstage with his signature smile and waved to the audience who applauded wildly. He let the applause go on until just the right moment and then stepped to the very front of the stage and said the line they were all waiting for, "How you doin?" The crowd went wild and the opening strains of *I Get a Kick Outta You* was Enzo's answer to the crowd appreciation.

Couples rose from their tables and headed out to the dance floor. David turned to Linda and asked, "Back when you and Bev first got this idea, did you ever think it would turn out like this? We are heading into the home stretch. Let's make the most of this!"

Linda smiled at David and rose to take his extended hand. They headed out to the dance floor and joined the other couples swaying to the music. No, she could not have dreamed that it would turn out like this. She only hoped that their efforts would be enough to make a difference.

. . . .

After the concert, the crowd was still buzzing about the performance. Enzo had delivered ninety minutes of pure energy and it was exactly what was needed to bring the crowd into the final hours of the fundraiser.

The smells of breakfast cooking got everyone headed to the buffet lines which offered a full breakfast of eggs, waffles, pancakes, and a selection of pastries. At one end, chefs prepared omlettes made to order and there were spiral hams with hash browns or scalloped potatoes for those with hearty appetites.

Linda took a moment to read Matt's latest text to the group about the latest election results. It was taking a long time to get final counts from several of the states. Results in Michigan were not final and a question about voter suppression had been raised. Also, results from some counties outside Philadelphia County in Pennsylvania were not falling into line with some of the pundit projections.

Election officials in all states had been on high alert for any voting irregularities and were cautious about announcing results. This was to be expected considering all that was at stake in the country this election. In the last presidential election, there had been confirmed instances of Russia using social media to influence the election. Driscoll's campaign had been accused of meddling and trying to influence voters, by trolling the other candidate and misrepresenting facts. Linda remembered all these events as she walked through the buffet and selected a waffle and scrambled eggs. Linda would have a quick breakfast and then begin her escape.

The decision had been made that each member of the team would leave the building on their own to avoid drawing attention. All communication would be by text so they could still be in touch if anyone had a problem. If anyone was delayed or worse – caught by someone and confronted, they all would not be caught. Since Matt was not leaving LF, he and Miguel would be the last people onsite. They had already packed up most of the monitors and moved them out to the van. At 6:45 they would pull the last plug, leave by the service entrance and drive back to the LF property as if nothing was amiss.

As the clock ticked closer to 6:00 am OL time, Linda went back to the command center. She and David would meet at 6:30 in the parking lot behind the building where he had parked their rental car. She found her overnight bag in the command center and wheeled it into the ladies' room without seeing anyone. She quickly changed out of her evening wear and into a casual outfit that would not attract attention and help her to blend in with crowds. She stuffed her gown and heels into the bag and put on her glasses and a gray baseball cap. She headed down the hallway toward the service entrance at the back.

As she rounded the corner to reach the back door, she stopped short. Jose Martinez was standing there waiting. He slowly walked towards her without saying a word.

Linda's mind quickly evaluated her options. Should she run? It was impossible to tell what he wanted.

"I have been watching Bev over the last few months as she works on this fundraiser," Jose began. "Tonight, I am justified in my suspicions.

Something is going on here. Marisol and I have talked about it and we want to know from you – what is really going on tonight?"

Linda quickly evaluated the situation and decided to go with the truth. "Jose, I want you to know that there is nothing happening that will hurt you, Marisol or Miquel."

"I was just outside, and I know it is already evening. It is not morning, the clock in my car says it is already Tuesday night." said Jose.

"Yes, you're right Jose. The truth is, we are not raising funds to elect Driscoll, we are trying to do exactly the opposite. We are hoping that this fundraiser will mislead enough people that they will not be able to vote and it will sway the election in favor of Governor Butler."

Jose slowly nodded his head. "I know Bev is a good person and since you are her best friend, Marisol and I wanted to trust that you would not do anything to hurt Miguel. But this plan is beyond what we imagined."

"Jose, we could not let everyone know all of our plans. It was too important to keep information as quiet as possible both to give our plan the best chance of success and to protect people helping us. It gives you deniability."

Jose shifted his weight and waited for Linda to explain further.

"Now, you can honestly say you didn't know what we were doing. It will protect your jobs at LF." Linda took a quick look at her watch and saw that it was 6:41. David was waiting for her.

"I see, now I want to know one more thing – did your plan work?"

Linda smiled, "That is the million-dollar question. We aren't sure even now. All I know is, we did our part and gave it our best shot. Now we will have to see how it plays out."

Jose smiled. "Well, now a lot of things make more sense. We trust you and Bev, and you can count on us to help with anything else you need."

Linda reached out her hand. Jose nodded again and gravely shook it to seal their pact.

"We can't thank you enough Jose. Today, we will make our escape since there is no telling what the fallout will be with everyone on LF. Maybe you can keep your eyes and ears open and give us the view from inside on what everyone says about this once they find out."

"Of course, we will be in touch with Matt." Jose smiled. "It is like they say – an audacious plan!"

Linda waved goodbye again and ran for the door. By most standards, the evening had been a huge success. Jose was one of the first to learn the truth. Linda was starting to feel a huge sense of relief. Nothing else mattered now, they had pulled off Operation Lifesaver. People had a wonderful evening and were now finishing up breakfast and were ready to head home and then go out to vote. Soon, they all would know the truth.

The drive to Tampa was a complete blur to Bev. Ruthie made sure that Bev's ankle was elevated and iced, and Bev was comfortable propped up among the bags of clean laundry. Her ankle throbbed but the pain was no match to the overwhelming fatigue. She dozed off while listening to Juanita and Ruthie chat as they made their way west across the state. Juanita was eager to hear the whole story; she had known of course that the Convention Center was hosting a large event but nothing beyond that.

Bev woke up a few hours later disoriented and confused. The truck had stopped but not at the airport as Bev had been expecting. Bev tried to maneuver so that she could see where they were but any movement at all caused the pain in her ankle to flare up.

"Mom just lie still. We're at the hospital- I want to get that ankle checked out. There's no way you can get on a plane tonight, so I've rearranged our plans. We'll make sure you didn't break anything and then we'll stay overnight here in Tampa and fly out tomorrow. Uncle Matt is bringing our suitcases to the hotel early tomorrow morning." Bev just nodded. She knew it was futile to argue with Ruthie and it did sound like a prudent plan.

A few hours later Bev was wheeled out of the ER with a heavily wrapped ankle, a prescription for painkillers and a set of crutches. Blessedly the ankle was not broken, just badly sprained. She was surprised to see that Juanita had not yet left.

"I promised my cousin that I would see you get on that plane. But now I'll help you get settled at the hotel. Besides there is no way I am leaving before I hear the full story. This is more exciting than any TV show. You guys should write a book. By the way, Miguel sends you a big hug. Everyone has been really worried about you"

"They needn't worry. I've been in excellent hands between you and Ruthie and I can't thank you enough. Now let's get to the hotel so I can finally get out of this damn dress."

Bev woke up early the next morning. She had slept reasonably well thanks to the painkillers. It was hard to believe that after 16 months of planning, worrying and scheming the entire thing was over. She looked across the room to where Ruthie, wearing the sweatpants and T shirt that she had purchased at the local Walmart, was sleeping. After Ruthie had made sure Bev was safely installed in bed with her foot elevated and a fresh ice bag, she and Juanita had gone back out to purchase some clothes, toothbrushes and an assortment of salads along with several pints of Ben and Jerry's. Bev had been hoping for a bottle of wine, but Ruthie had emphatically said that no way was Bev to mix alcohol with her pain meds. Bev had very reluctantly agreed.

The three spread the feast across the beds and turned on the TV, anxious to catch the election results and even more anxious to see if Operation Lifesaver had worked. By this time Ruthie and Juanita, both the same age and both determined and driven young women, had become fast friends. Juanita now felt that she was an official member of the Operation Lifesaver team and just as vested in the results.

At 7:30 PM, CNN had reported that it was a close race in Florida with unexpected results in Sumter County. It was reported that Sumter County, a traditionally Republican stronghold, was leaning towards Governor Butler. Fifteen minutes later it was definite - Sumter County, which included Leisure Falls, was going Democratic in the presidential election. Ruthie and Juanita leapt to their feet in exultation while Bev waved a crutch victoriously. It had worked. The plan hatched on a Danube River cruise sixteen months ago had actually worked!

Bev tried to reach Linda, but the call went straight to voicemail- they were probably still on their flight home. Although she dearly wanted to celebrate that moment with her best friend, Bev knew that she would see her up in Wisconsin the next evening. Bev hoped that they would then have even more to celebrate.

Several hours later, after the Ben and Jerrys was entirely consumed, Juanita left for home. She and Ruthie vowed to stay in touch, Ruthie urging Juanita to come visit her in the Windy City. Bev once again thank Juanita for coming to her rescue, giving her as fierce a hug as she could manage on crutches.

And then the remaining returns for Florida became official. The giddy feelings of victory were replaced by incredulous disappointment. Even with the Sumter County votes for Butler, somehow the state of Florida ended up as a win for Driscoll. Even the CNN analyst seemed at a loss since, in the past, the Sumter County votes were usually a reliable measure of the way Florida as a state would vote. But not this time.

Bev hobbled as quietly as possible across the hotel room to make some morning coffee, thinking back on last night and trying not to wake Ruthie. Exhaustion had finally overtaken them both and they had fallen asleep knowing that Florida's electoral votes were going to Driscoll. None of the news stations had been anywhere near prepared to make a declaration regarding who would be sitting in the Oval Office next year. When Bev had checked her phone first thing upon waking that morning, the situation hadn't changed. The network analysts were anticipating that a decision on the whole election would be announced later that night.

Ruthie stirred and sat up. "Coffee smells good. Got a cup for me?"

Bev and Ruthie sipped their coffee in silence. They were both still tired from the ordeal of the last few days and subdued from the devastating news of the Florida results. Neither of them could drum up the energy to point out that returns were still being counted and recounted in various states across the country; the national election was not yet over. A couple of quiet taps on the door broke the stillness.

Bev opened the door to find both Matt and Edna. Matt set down a white bakery box on the table.

"Brought you some breakfast Sis-some scones and Danish. I've got your car with your luggage ready to go downstairs. Edna followed me in her car. We'll drop you off at the airport and then Edna can drive me back." Matt took a closer look at Bev and examined her foot. "Jeez Bev, that ankle looks pretty swollen. You had better keep icing it." He took a big bite from a cherry

Danish. "Ruthie, how are you doing this morning? Did you have a good time at the fundraiser with all those oldsters? It sure wasn't dull and what an exit your mom made. From the way things look this morning, I think you were smart to take her to the hospital."

Ruthie made another pot of coffee and the four of them sat down to enjoy the breakfast and debrief on the events of the previous night. Bev spoke up first -she couldn't wait any longer to find out just how involved Edna had been.

"Edna you knew all along? You knew that we were trying to keep the Leisure Falls community away from the polls?"

"Yes, I figured it out quite early actually. I really didn't think it would work but it all sounded like such fun. I was so happy to be in on it - life has been very humdrum for me these last years and it's been grand getting to know your brother."

Bev turned to Matt, "What was Grimes doing there and was he actually helping us? I couldn't believe my eyes when he dragged Eric off the stage- I'm really confused about all that".

Matt chuckled "You'd better ask Edna, Sis. That was all her doing."

Edna, blushing a bit, preceded to tell an astonished Bev and Ruthie how she and Nelson Grimes had been involved for almost a decade, romantically involved that is.

"I know he acts the buffoon but deep inside he is a very sensitive and spiritual man."

Bev and Ruth both had their mouths open, dumbfounded.

Edna continued, unperturbed by their reaction "Nell has always been proud of what he calls his little booby traps that he would program into his software. As smart as your brother is with computers, I was worried that he would unknowingly set off a few and all his plans - all our plans- would go helter skelter. So, I called him in Russia."

Ruthie, fascinated by this tale of hidden romance and intrigue sputtered "What did he say when you called?"

"He said he would come home immediately of course."

"And it's a good thing he did, "Matt interjected. "I would have unknowingly set off half a dozen traps- there's no saying what would have happened. I can't believe I didn't see anything fishy. Grimes is much better at this stuff than I had originally assessed.' Matt looked embarrassed.

"Matt, I have told you over and over, you can't blame yourself. Who would imagine that a security system at a retirement community would be so laden with traps? That's Nell's way of having fun. Nell stayed at my house the last two nights out of sight, just keeping an eye on things- he was able to interface with the security monitors Matt had set up and of course he disengaged all the traps. Unfortunately, he unknowingly compromised the Internet dead zone Matt had installed which is how Eric got involved. When Nell saw what Eric was up to, he knew he had to take immediate action."

Edna started laughing. "It's ironic that my two favorite men, both IT masters, have been working at cross purposes. All this effort to pull this off and you geniuses could have sabotaged the whole thing with your fancy software maneuvers."

Bev broke in "So Grimes wanted our plan to succeed? He wants Driscoll to lose?"

"Oh, he really doesn't care too much about politics dear, but he knew this whole thing had become important to me. Nell was happy that I had found a bit of excitement, something to keep me occupied- I tend to get muzzy in the brain when I'm bored."

Bev and Ruth just sat in stunned silence, letting Edna's story sink in.

Finally, Bev spoke up. "Matt, do you have an idea what happened with the Florida vote? After we won Sumter County, I thought that Florida would go to Butler."

"The latest news is that the Florida governor invalidated the votes cast by felons who have not yet payed their fines These would likely have been votes for Butler. There was talk that an emergency Florida Supreme Court hearing would be scheduled for today but now it doesn't look like that will happen. But don't lose hope yet; there is news that Driscoll is not getting the same support from rural areas across the country as he did in the last election. We just have to sit tight. Let's get you over to the airport; it might take you awhile to get to your gate on those crutches. Maybe we can get you a lift on one of those golf carts they have."

On the way to the airport, Matt filled Bev in on what happened when the event ended, and people discovered that it was 7:00 PM and the polls were closed.

"About half of them were furious and the other half were just plain confused. And it was like we figured, no one wanted to complain to the voting commission. They were too embarrassed to explain how they partied their way through an entire Election Day. No fingers have been pointed towards you... yet but Eric, as committee head, is getting plenty of heat and he'll be looking to pass the blame. I think it is just a matter of time before they bring up your name. But Bev, and don't take offense here, I don't think anyone will believe that you, my scatter-brained big sis, masterminded a scheme of this complexity. Linda and Ruthie stayed in the shadows so their involvement is unknown."

Matt thought it all over again to see if he had changed his opinion from his early impressions. "Actually, I'm pretty sure that Eric will do everything to sweep this under the rug and deflect attention. He keeps boasting about how successful the fundraiser was for Driscoll and the Republican Party. According to him the event raised 2 1/2 million dollars. That's what he'll keep trumpeting. I also heard that there will be fireworks tonight if Driscoll wins."

Bev hoped that what Matt said was true. Even though she was unlikely to ever set foot in Leisure Falls again, she still cringed at the thought that she might be the focus of the entire community's animosity.

At the airport, Matt was able to arrange for a cart to carry Bev, Ruthie and their luggage to the gate. They boarded and settled themselves in an aisle with an empty middle seat. As their plane took off, bound for Chicago, Ruthie squeezed her mother's hand.

"I am so so proud of you and Aunt Linda. No matter what Mom, you really did pull it off. The whole thing was a big success. You two had this crazy plan and you did it. Wait till Aunt Linda hears about your escape with the laundry. I wish I had thought to take a picture. "

The trip back home had been uneventful. Even though she and Bev had put the Operation Lifesaver timeline together, It had been a little disorienting to be in the middle of the fundraiser where the OL time was 6:30 am and then stepping out into the parking lot where Linda was immediately hit with the realization that it was really 6:30 pm. She had to chuckle to herself – how funny that she had even managed to fool herself! Once they were at the airport, Linda and David relaxed and waited at the gate for their 8:30 pm flight. Television monitors blared the latest news about the election results. Even now, results were not final. At 8:00 as they were boarding their flight, the Broward county votes were finalized, and Driscoll's 16,000 vote lead had evaporated. With 90% of the votes in, Butler was ahead.

As their flight left Florida, Linda wondered if they would know the outcome by the time they landed. Even without any sleep, she was too keyed up to rest on the flight. She tried to distract herself by watching a movie and was only mildly successful. Every time she looked at her watch, no more than 15 minutes had passed. The three-hour flight seemed to take an eternity, but when they were finally off the plane, Linda saw a huge crowd gathered in the terminal looking at the CNN report of election results. David and Linda joined the edge of the crowd to see the latest.

"With Florida now firmly in the Driscoll column, the final results from Texas and Arizona will decide the election. This is good news for

Driscoll since those states have been reliably Republican, but CNN is still saying that those states are too close to call."

Linda took a deep breath and tried to absorb the full impact of this news. She was shocked to finally hear that they had lost, even though she knew it had been a long shot for Florida to go to the democratic candidate. All that work, all their plans, it had all been so perfect that Linda had let herself believe they had made a difference. She could not imagine living through another four years of Driscoll as the president of the United States. She felt utterly defeated and disappointed beyond belief. If there was anyone who felt worse, it was probably Bev. Linda wanted to call her, but she thought Bev was probably either sleeping or on a plane – or both.

"I knew it was too good to be true when Driscoll's lead disappeared. They cheat in Florida every time. This time, I thought our efforts would be enough to make the difference in vote count, but there is no accounting for other schemes the party will pull to influence the outcome."

Recently Linda had read about The Sentencing Project which estimated that, as of 2016, approximately 6.1 million people or 2.5 percent of the U.S. voting age population, were disenfranchised due to a felony conviction. Florida's disenfranchised felons made up 10% of the adult population, and 21.5% of the adult African American population. In 2018, Florida voters decided this was not right and passed the largest expansion of American voting rights in decades, a state constitutional amendment that allowed most ex-felons to vote in elections. This gave nearly 10 percent of voting-aged adults, the right to vote again — a key swing state that Driscoll won by less than 113,000 votes in 2016 and George

W. Bush by 537 votes in 2000. For the 2020 election, there had been lawsuits and much political maneuvering to limit voting rights for felons even though the voters had spoken. Sadly, it appeared that this was a key factor again, with enough to give Driscoll Florida.

"I know that is not the outcome we wanted for Florida, but the election is not over yet. Let's catch our limo and watch from home." David said. "I'm actually a little surprised that both Texas and Arizona are still undecided".

Although the outcome was still not final, it was a huge disappointment that all their efforts were not enough. Linda suddenly felt exhausted and let David guide her to their waiting limo. When the door shut and they pulled away from the terminal, the silence in the car matched how Linda felt – entirely deflated and empty. Her phone vibrated and she saw Bev's picture appear. She picked up the call.

"Where are you?" Linda asked.

"I'm fine, there was some drama in my escape, but I'm ok now. You will never believe what happened. "Bev was out of breath and apparently had not yet heard the news about Florida.

"I'm glad you are ok; we'll have to catch each other up on the details of our escape. Did you hear the news about Florida?"

"Yes, I just heard. Once again, Florida went for Driscoll in the end. There is talk of a recount, and I'm sure there was some kind of cheating involved. But, let's not forget it's not over yet. I still have my fingers crossed for a miracle." Bev sounded as tired as Linda felt.

"When does your flight land?" Linda asked.

"We are staying in Tampa tonight, it's a long story. I should be at the lake by 4:00 tomorrow afternoon. It's a good thing Ruthie is with me, I'm not sure how I feel, and it is a little disorienting to try to pick up my life after all that we have been through. My emotions are all over the place. On one hand, I feel drained like I could sleep for a week, but then I remember the election isn't over yet. It seemed like Operation Lifesaver would work. I can't really believe it is over and that it didn't work."

"Yes, that is exactly how I feel too – drained, but still anxious about what we are going to find out next." Linda stared out the window of the car as the driver easily pushed past the speed limit to what felt like 100 miles per hour. Ordinarily it would make Linda's hands sweat just to think about how fast they were going, but this time she did not have the energy even for that.

"Have a good flight, we will see you tomorrow at the lake and will have a nice dinner ready. I am so ready for this to be over. We will have time to debrief on what happened at the fundraiser and by then, maybe we will know who our next president is." Linda switched off the phone and spent the next 45 minutes imagining how she would feel when she heard the final election results. David scanned the news on his phone but didn't say anything more. They both sat in silence with their own thoughts.

As they pulled into the driveway, Linda exhaled a sign of relief. Coming home had never felt so good. Groceries had been delivered and after a light snack of tuna salad, Linda and David sat on the patio around the firepit for a few minutes. Fall was in the air. It was a cool clear night and it felt wonderful to sit quietly and absorb the energy. Somehow, life would go on even if Driscoll won the election, and as the night wore on, Linda began to feel more grounded again and reminded herself they could still be optimistic. It was getting very late and Linda finally felt ready to get some sleep. They headed into bed and slept deeply.

By Wednesday morning, election results were still not final. Several key counties were still not completely counted leaving the final results for the states too close to call. Networks were being very careful to avoid making a mistake and as a result, there was lots of opinions and predictions, but no final results. All day long Linda and David alternately watched the news reporting and left the TV to try to relax outside. The waiting was hard to take.

At 3:40 pm, David came out to the patio with a hot cup of tea for Linda and consulted his watch. "You will be glad to know that Arizona and Texas are close to calling it – probably at the top of the hour, which is in only 20 minutes."

Just then, they heard a car horn honking in the driveway. It was Bev and Ruthie announcing their arrival. Linda and David hurried to the front and found Bev and Ruthie getting bags and crutches out of the trunk. Linda welcomed them both with a big long hug.

Bev brushed off Linda's alarm over her taped-up ankle, "It was a stupid accident and I'm fine. I'll fill you in later."

"It is so good to see you both and your timing is perfect. They will be announcing the latest results for Texas and Arizona at 4:00." Linda said.

"This is it then isn't it?" Bev looked at Linda with resolve in her eyes.

"Well, let's hurry up inside and see what they have to say." Ruthie encouraged them all up the driveway. They all dumped the bags in the foyer and headed into the family room.

"Ok, let's go in to get the news." Linda's stomach clenched hoping this would be the outcome she wanted. As she walked into the house and began to settle herself in front of the TV, she flashed back to the moment 4 years ago when they thought there would be a first woman president. Linda could still relive the shock and surprise of losing that day and of hearing the reporters announce the impossible – Driscoll had been elected. They all settled themselves in front of the TV and waited for the announcement.

The breaking news headline splashed across the screen and Barry Jones appeared at the news desk along with the whole team reporting on the election results. A whiteboard map of the United States was colored in with the results for each state creating a picture of blue and red.

Barry Jones leaned into the camera. "I think we finally have the news many of you have been waiting for. With the results being closer than expected, the experts and analytic staff have taken the precaution to rerun and verify all the returns. As each county reports, our team rechecks this against our database of expected votes and likely voters."

"Let's get to the bottom line!" Linda roared at the TV. They all sat immobile and not breathing wanting to hear and yet not wanting the bad news.

"NBC has the final results to report from the last two states, Texas and Arizona. With 98% of the vote in, NBC analysts have made the call for the state of Texas for Governor Butler. All 38 electoral votes will be awarded to Governor Butler." On the big board, Texas was filled in with blue and the smiling face of Governor Butler. The total count of electoral votes automatically updated to show Butler now with 279 and Driscoll with 243.

"Take that Driscoll!" David howled, jumping up and jabbing his finger at the TV screen, reminding Linda of the time his White Sox won the World Series in 2005. At that time, she had never seen him so happy, now David was every bit as focused on a win as he was then. It would all come down to the last state Arizona.

Late last night a group from Michigan had registered a complaint about voter suppression in Wayne County, the county that included Detroit and over 1 million voters. Election officials had investigated the complaint that polls had closed early, while voters still waited in lines. This had caused a delay in reporting final results, but now Linda could see that Michigan had been added to Butler's column. Another victory in a state that Driscoll won last time by only a few votes.

While their efforts had been focused on Florida, Linda and Bev had also hoped that, when it came down to it, voters in many states would be dissatisfied with Driscoll's leadership and turn away from him. Many blue-collar workers had not done well with Driscoll and his constant attacks on the Affordable Care Act, post office, worker rights to organize and tariff wars where bailout money went to large agribusiness and support for small and family farmers never materialized.

Linda returned her attention to Barry Jones. "Also, with 97% of the votes in, NBC is making the call for Arizona and all of the 11 electoral votes for the state of Arizona will go to Governor Butler."

They all looked at each other in disbelief. The final electoral count was Driscoll – 243 and Butler 295. Even with Florida going to Driscoll, the American people had spoken, previously red and purple states had emerged as blue giving Butler the victory with 295 electoral votes.

"In the end, you and Linda were not the only ones who had had enough of Driscoll and his brand of politics." Ruthie said, smiling broadly.

"Your work in Florida was important, but you can see there was a wave of blue that came across the country. This election took those bastards right out of office in the White House and in the Senate. Driscoll's loss went down the ticket and now the Democrats have both the House and the Senate. It's time to put our house back in order. As Gerald Ford once said, "Our long national nightmare is over!" David raised his fists triumphantly.

"This calls for a celebration! I'll get the champagne. I kept a bottle on ice just in case…" Linda said smiling broadly. She returned and passed out the flutes with bubbling rose champagne.

Bev raised her glass for a toast, "You can never leave democracy up to someone else. It's easy to think there is nothing you can do compared to all the powerful bigwigs. The past is history, the future a mystery, but today is a gift because of the voters that finally showed up" - she paused and smiled "and those that didn't."

"Cheers!" They all savored the toast and watched the TV for a while as scenes from around the country revealed the festive atmosphere.

"It's hard to absorb all the implications of this." Linda said. "It will take me a while to wrap my brain around all of this. For now, I am going to enjoy the victory. Our work is done, and we can get on with our lives."

"My life is really changing – leaving LF and coming back up north. What will we spend our time doing now that Operation Lifesaver is over?" Bev asked Linda.

"I'm not sure, but I have a few ideas to talk over with you." Linda said.

A big thank you to all who contributed their time, energy, and ideas. Thanks to Robin Locke Monda who designed the beautiful cover. Thanks also to Scott, Beth, John, Lori, and Randy.

A special thank you to Keith.

Epilogue

Many significant events were happening in the US during the writing of this book. When we started writing, we were all feeling the exhaustion of living though daily press conferences and tweet storms but also some major outrages leaving many people no option but to tune out the news to preserve their sanity. In October of 2019, an impeachment inquiry began but no one was sure that these revelations would bring different results. Some did believe that, this time, our government would work as designed and even if Trump was not removed from office, he would suffer the shame of impeachment and we would at least have documented the unacceptability of his actions to set a precedent for the future.

We realized that removing him from office would not totally solve the problem. He is one rotten apple, but there are many more and if we continue this course, someone will come along that is worse. This book was a fictional account of an example of the activism that is needed from leaders and citizens to ensure that our democracy continues to survive. Every day, lives of many people continue seemingly unchanged, but lurking beneath the surface, out of sight for now, is the very real danger of authoritarianism and if left unchecked even fascism.

It was not that long ago the world learned the cost of letting this kind of behavior go for too long. In the US, we like to think the good guys will win in the end, that they have God and destiny as an exceptional nation on our side. But the truth is, we are as vulnerable to corruption, prejudice and evil as anyone else. It starts as a slow trickle, not really hurting anything, but annoying. Then it builds to the point where there are consequences for some economically, physically and emotionally. Eventually, left unchecked, a tipping point is reached and if there is no intervention, the infection will break open and spread.

There is no medicine for this infection other than the light of truth and the courage to act. Dystopian stories are intriguing partly because we think the outrageousness cannot happen in real life. But we are not immune to the dangers of political catastrophe and there are no guarantees that government will always be by the people and for the people. Will future societies look back on this 250-year period as a blip in time, as a grand experiment that ultimately failed, as proof that all forms of government are ultimately corrupt? Certainly, other great civilizations have lasted much longer. Will people believe that capitalism was ultimately just as corrupt as communism – in the 1980's we celebrated being so superior to this failed experiment – and that democracy is a weak form of government easily susceptible to failure given enough time and just the wrong human factors?

Speaking of infection and immunity, this book was also written at the time the coronavirus was rampaging throughout the world. It hit hard in the US in March and soon mayors and governors were making the tough decisions to order shutdowns of schools and businesses. "Social distancing" practices became the norm for everyone. Teachers moved all face-to-face education to online in a mere two weeks over the spring break. Workers learned to telecommute and new tools such as Zoom and FaceTime allowed friends and family members to stay somewhat connected even if they could no longer be physically together. Hospitals, physician, nurses and first responders prepared for the surge of patients that would need to be hospitalized.

This crisis further exposed the incompetence of Trump. COVID-19 was not susceptible to "The Art of The Deal". This was a crisis he could not escape by calling it a hoax or fake news. It was real – and it kept unfolding as the days went by. At each press briefing, Trump made promises he did not keep (testing, protective gear, ventilators). He tested the patience of every scientist and public health official by denying the facts, talking about untested medications that could be used and projecting arbitrary dates by which he wanted the crisis to end (Easter).

The financial crisis that accompanied the virus was very real too. However, this became the primary focus for Trump and while he failed to recognize the seriousness of the virus, his lack of empathy for the people of the US was on display every day. Coronavirus was a crisis beyond his capability and surviving it will depend on the strength, ingenuity and resilience of the people themselves. We will get through it, not due to federal leadership, but despite Trump and everyone will have to decide to jump in, take action and do their part in the absence of his leadership. We could not have written a story as compelling as the real events that unfolded each day, but they served to underscore the point of this book.

The true outcomes remain unknown at this point. As we approach the 2020 election, it looks like there will be an unrelenting effort to suppress the vote. As an example of what is to come, Wisconsin held its primary election in April and Republicans refused to expand mail-in voting leaving many voters standing in lines for hours to exercise their right to vote.

Hopefully, the right thing happens and, in the end, all Americans will get involved and get out to vote in November.

Made in the USA
Monee, IL
24 July 2020